THE DRAGON KEEPER

THE ILLUSIA CHRONICLES
BOOK 2

DIANE MARTIN

Copyright © 2024 by Diane Martin. All rights reserved. Grand Prairie, Texas USA

No part of this publication may be reproduced, distributed, or transmitted in any form or by any means, including photocopying, recording, or other electronic or mechanical methods, without the prior written permission of the publisher, except as permitted by U.S. copyright law. For permission requests, email dianemartin@dianemartinbooks.com.

The story, all names, characters, and incidents portrayed in this production are fictitious. No identification with actual persons (living or deceased), places, buildings, and products is intended or should be inferred.

Book cover and illustrations by Joshua Martin (Instagram @theartkidd).

ISBN for paperback: 978-1-957854-02-1; ISBN for hardback: 978-1-957854-03-8

Library of Congress Control Number: 2024904642

Visit the author's website: https://dianemartinbooks.com

For those who call me Didi

I hope you'll always choose joy.

Chapter 1

"Roooar! I am a scary dragon, and I'm going to gobble you up!" I growled to my little sister as she sat in the tall yellow grass. I leaned toward her with my fingers outstretched, my face wearing a scary scowl.

Before I could grab her, Kate ran down the hill screaming, her brown ponytail coming undone as she ran.

"Papa! Papa! The dragon's going to eat me!"

Our father turned from the back of the horse-drawn wagon where he'd been cleaning his farm tools. His eyes grew wide, searching as he looked behind her. Kate ran into his legs, nearly knocking him over. She wrapped her arms around his knees, burying her head in his trousers.

Pa frowned when his eyes landed on me. "Zander, come down here right now!" he called as he removed his wide-brimmed work hat and wiped his brow.

Tucking my hands in my pockets, I met him at the bottom of the hill. "Yes, sir?" I kept my head down. I hated disappointing my father.

Pa let out a long breath as he pried Kate's arms from his legs. He gently turned her around to face me. "Your brother has something to say to you," he said to Kate.

"I do?" I bit my lower lip.

Pa glared at me, his dark bushy eyebrows separated only by a deep wrinkle. Sweat and dirt covered his tanned face.

"Oh, right. I do." I paused to think about what I should say and crouched down to meet Kate's eyes. She twirled a lock of hair around her finger—something she did when she was nervous or frightened. "I'm sorry I scared you." I stood but heard Pa clear his throat—a sure sign that he wasn't satisfied. "Um..., I shouldn't have done that." I glanced up at him, but he continued to wait expectantly, so I added more. "Drake's part of our family, and you should never be afraid of him. Okay?"

Kate nodded slowly as a grin spread across her face. She lifted her head and said to Pa, "I was only pretending to be scared. He didn't really scare me."

Pa's hand swept through his hair in a tired gesture, followed by the familiar placement of his hat. We both had the same wavy hair. Ma used to say I would grow up looking just like him.

Pa turned back to the wagon. "Kate, go on down to the cottage while I talk to Zander for a bit."

Oh no. Pa had that tone in his voice—the one he used when I was in trouble but didn't know it yet.

"Yes, Papa," she said and skipped away from us, her long messy hair bobbing behind her.

I waited quietly until my father was ready to speak.

Letting out a breath, Pa turned around, a gentleness in his eyes. "Son, do you remember what your ma always said?" He gently squeezed my shoulder. "Choose joy. Remember?"

"I remember, Pa." Ma had stitched those words on cloth and tacked it to the wall near the fireplace. I saw it every day and thought about her each time.

"Did you choose joy?"

"Yes, sir," I answered. Kate and I had been having fun.

"No, son, I don't think you did. At least, not for your sister. Even though she said she was pretending, that scream sounded pretty real. Remember that she's a tenderhearted six-year-old. You're twelve—almost a man. It's your job to watch out for her." He leaned down to look in my eyes. "And take care that you don't ever give her a reason to fear Drake. He's family—Buddy, too—and Kate needs to know she's always safe with them." He stood up, his gaze sweeping over the field. "We owe Drake so much. Remember what he did for us."

I'd heard the story so many times. I held in a sigh.

"Speaking of Drake," he continued, "have you checked on him today? Changed his bandage? Made sure he has plenty of water and fresh hay?"

My face grew hot. The day had flown by. I couldn't remember if I had checked on him yesterday, either. "No, sir. I guess I felt like he was doing all right now."

"He's not there yet. Do I need to remind you that you're the reason he's in the barn recovering?" He paused until I shook my head. "I handle the feeding, and you handle everything else. That was our arrangement. Keep tending to him until he's back to normal. Just a few more days."

"Yes, sir."

Pa gave a single nod. "Okay then. It's about time for dinner," he said over his shoulder as he turned to the wagon. "You go on back to the cottage and get it started, and I'll be along after I put my tools in the barn."

"Can't I stay out for a little bit longer? It's not dark yet."

Pa's stomach growled and gurgled. He grinned. "You hear that?

That means it's time to eat. I'm sure Kate's hungry, too, even if you aren't." He tilted his head and raised an eyebrow as he waited for my response. That look always meant the conversation was over.

"Yes, Pa."

I shoved my hands in my pockets as I walked to our little white house. Kate sat in her Kate-sized rocking chair on the wooden porch, holding her tattered doll in her arms.

"I'm hungry," she mumbled when I reached the porch.

"I know. I'm working on it." I clenched my jaw to prevent any hurtful words from bursting out.

"I'm sorry I got you in trouble." She rubbed her ear and slowly looked up at me. "Are you mad at me?" She lifted her doll and said in a silly fake voice, "Yeah, we're sorry. Don't be mad."

A smile tugged at my lips. I could never stay mad at her for long. "You're quite the actor, you know? You even had *me* fooled."

She giggled.

I turned and cupped my hands to my mouth. "Buddy!" I called. "Here, Buddy!"

I heard the familiar bark, which always made me smile. Buddy ran out of the woods that bordered the edge of our farmland, ears folded back, mouth open with his tongue flopping out to the side. It made him look like he was smiling. The dog barely slowed down before he reached the porch.

Kate dropped to her knees and gave Buddy a hug, her hands disappearing in the dog's thick white fur. She was repaid with a slobbery lick and a wagging tail. Kate giggled. "I love you, too, Buddy. Did you have a fun day? Yeah?"

Inside the cottage, Kate went into our shared bedroom while I started dinner. Buddy stood nearby, waiting for the usual scraps.

"No, Buddy," I said as I carefully sliced the cured ham. The dog wagged his curly tail in response to his name, his eyes black with anticipation. "You already ate. Besides, Pa says you're getting fat 'cause I'm giving you too many snacks. Go lay down."

Buddy let out a short whine and plopped down on his blanket next to the table.

I set a loaf of bread on the cutting board. Kate hummed a tune in the bedroom, no doubt putting her doll to sleep. Ma used to hum as she worked, and it always made me smile when I heard Kate singing the same songs.

I was torn from my thoughts when Buddy's ears perked up, his head tilting back and forth as he looked at the back window. A low growl rumbled in his throat. His body tensed.

Kate came out of her room, her rag doll cradled in her arm. "What is it, Buddy?"

The dog sprang into action, letting out a series of sharp barks. Tail stiff and alert, he paced back and forth.

Kate's eyes grew in concern as loud shouts came through the wall of the house. I could hear Pa's voice among them, but there were two other voices I didn't recognize. We ran to the back window to see what was happening.

Pa stood protectively in front of the large barn doors, his double-sided ax held firmly in front of him. He stood with his legs spread apart, his body tense and ready for a fight. Two men stood across from him, their backs to us. One pointed a sword at Pa, and the other held a coil of rope in his hand. Both men wore long black coats and black hats.

"Who are they?" Kate asked, her fingers twirling a strand of hair as her other hand clutched her doll.

I slowly shook my head in silent answer as we stood gaping at the scene.

What could those men want?

Buddy whined and pawed at the door, begging to get out—ready to guard and protect his family.

I was torn; one part of me wanted to rush out and help Pa, but the other part knew he'd want me to stay inside and keep my sister safe. My heart raced as I struggled with what to do.

The man with the rope yelled something at Pa and pointed at the barn doors. Pa angrily shook his head, and the man punched him in the stomach. Kate screamed. Pa doubled over in pain but swung his ax at his attackers even before straightening up. They jumped back, staying just out of reach. Pa coughed, his body wrenching from the effort.

Before I could stop her, Kate ran to the door. "Get 'em, Buddy!" she yelled.

The door had barely opened before Buddy forced his way out, disappearing around the corner.

"Kate, stay inside!" I commanded as I watched from the window. Buddy came into view, barking ferociously, his hackles raised as he raced to the barn.

Kate stood beside me at the window. She grabbed my hand and held it with a fierce grip.

Buddy charged at the intruders and clamped his jaws around the nearest ankle. The man holding the rope let out a yell and frantically shook his leg, attempting to shake Buddy off. In desperation, he swung the coil of rope, striking Buddy repeatedly. The dog whimpered and released his grip, tumbling to the ground.

"No," I cried, my voice rough and choked.

Pa held his stomach, each cough wracking his body with pain. The swordsman roughly shoved him aside, causing Pa's ax to skitter out of reach as he hit the ground. The intruder flung open the barn doors and entered; his limping accomplice followed. From the ground, Pa shouted at them, punctuated by another series of coughs. Gathering his strength, he rose to his feet, snatched up his ax, and staggered into the barn after them.

Kate dropped her doll. "Drake's in there!" She ran across the room and out the door.

"Kate! Come back!" I yelled, not far behind her.

We were halfway to the barn when a fireball erupted through its open door. We froze in place, our eyes wide.

Terrified screams reached us from inside the building.

My whole body trembled. I couldn't breathe.

"Papa!" Kate wailed.

I grabbed her shoulders and turned her toward me. "Go to the well. Get water."

She ran behind the house while I sprinted toward the barn. I'd barely taken five steps when the barn's windows exploded. The force of the blast knocked me off my feet. Shards of shattered glass rained down. I squinted, lifting my arm to protect my face from the searing heat.

Buddy slowly rose to his feet and let out a determined bark before hurrying to the barn. No sooner had he vanished from sight than a section of the barn's wall gave way, collapsing in a fiery heap. Orange flames reached toward the sky.

"Buddy!" I screamed, my voice cracking. The barn gave an eerie moan just moments before the roof caved in. "No, no, no, no, no!"

Kate came into view, running as she carried the water bucket in front of her, the precious liquid sloshing down the front of her dress. I jumped up and grabbed her arm, spinning her around to shield her from the disastrous scene. The bucket fell from her hands as she fought to pull out of my grip.

"Nooo! We have to help Papa!" she shrieked.

The entire barn flared up as gray smoke billowed through the roof, the doors, the shattered windows.

The heat of the fire kept us from moving closer. Even from this distance, the blazing temperature stung my skin.

I stood, watching helplessly as I held Kate. My body had gone numb. It was all I could do to stay standing.

Pa was strong. He was smart. If there was a way out, he would find it.

Massive sobs overtook Kate's little body. Her wails hurt me deep inside. Tears streamed down my cheeks as I shook my head in disbelief.

This couldn't be happening.

It couldn't be real.

We didn't move. We *couldn't* move.

Kate's tears wet my shirt as I held her against me, my own tears falling into her hair. We just held each other and wept.

From the size of the blaze, we knew.

No one could have survived.

Chapter 2

"Whatcha doin', Zander?" Kate asked, out of breath from playing in the field with Buddy. The dog stood next to her, panting; his tongue flopped out of his mouth like a big, goofy pink flag waving in the breeze.

"Trying to fix this," I said. Standing hunched over Pa's workbench near the side of the house, I slammed down the hammer with more force than necessary. The handle for the water well had broken the day before, and I'd been trying to put it back together for over an hour.

Kate nudged in closer to see.

I complained, "Could you move over? You're blocking the sunlight. I can't see what I'm doing." I knew I shouldn't be taking my frustrations out on her, but I couldn't stop myself. I returned to my project and swung the hammer. "I just can't..." the hammer missed its mark "...get this nail..." the hammer missed again "...to go in." The hammer missed but nabbed the edge of my thumb. My chest tightened from the intense pain, and I shrieked, dropping the tool to the ground. I jumped up and down, holding my injured thumb.

"Are you okay?" Kate pulled on my arm to see my injury.

I roughly shook off her touch. "No, I am not okay!" I yelled, inches from her face.

I let out a growl as I picked up the hammer and threw it as far as I could, watching as it arced high over the field before falling out of sight. I bent over with a deep groan and clutched my throbbing thumb. The piercing spasm pulsed through my entire body. I had never experienced such pain before.

"Zander?" I could barely hear her voice above the heartbeat pounding in my ears.

"No, Kate! Just leave me alone." I turned my back to her, feeling like I would snap. "You have no idea how hard I'm working just to keep things running around here. I'm tired. I'm hungry. And I just can't do this!" I growled again and clenched my hair with my fingers.

Kate whimpered, taking quick, shallow breaths. I turned to apologize and caught a glimpse of her quivering chin just before she ran into the house, slamming the door behind her.

Buddy whined, his gaze going from me to the door and back again. He tilted his head as he looked at me. Just what I needed—criticism from the dog.

"I know, I know." I rubbed my face and sighed.

Kate had never looked at me with such fear. And I'd caused it. This wasn't like her fake scare from two weeks ago. This was real. Breathing deeply, I closed my eyes for a moment. My thumb pulsed, my body ached, and now my heart stung from what I had done.

There was always so much work to do on the farm. No time to rest. No time for fun. Not even time to feel sad about Pa's and Drake's deaths. I'd been the one in charge of everything since the fire. Kate and Buddy depended on me, and I couldn't let them down.

So much pressure.

The well handle taunted me, as if it knew I couldn't fix it. One thing was for sure: I wouldn't be able to finish the job without the hammer. Shaking my head, I walked to the field to search for it.

Pa had harvested most of the remaining crops shortly before the fire. I had always admired the straight lines he plowed so carefully. Pa knew how to do everything—grow crops, fix things, take care of the family—and he made it look effortless. Ma had died three years ago, and Pa must have been exhausted every single day since then, filling the role of both mother and father. *I* was exhausted, and I didn't do even half of what Pa did.

I missed him so much.

I swallowed the lump in my throat as I hunted for the hammer. When I finally found it, the thought of returning to my endless mental list of projects made me sag to the ground. The sadness that had been buried within me for two weeks welled up in my chest. I held my head in my hands, fighting to keep my emotions inside, but they burst out anyway. Tears flowed as sobs shook my body.

I had never felt so overwhelmed. So alone.

Something touched my ear, followed by a hot breath panting on my neck. I wiped my face on my sleeve as a smile tugged at my lips. Buddy whined and licked my cheek. I wrapped my arms around the dog's neck as he sank against me, his tail wagging happily. We sat like that for a while as I ran my fingers through his soft white fur.

"You're right," I whispered to my long-time friend. "I'm *not* alone, am I?"

Buddy pulled out of the hug and lay down next to me, licking his front paw which had been burned in the barn fire. I knew nothing about treating animal injuries, but he seemed to be taking care of it himself. He had moved slowly after the fire but appeared to have no long-term damage.

"Zander?" I looked over my shoulder, and there stood Kate, holding a plate with a big chunk of bread, more than one person could eat. She knelt beside me. "You said you were hungry." She avoided looking at me, which made my heart ache.

I took the plate and touched her arm in gratitude. "I'm sorry," I whispered, trying to keep my voice from shaking. I struggled to find the right words. "I'm sorry I yelled at you, and I'm sorry I got so angry and made you scared. It'll never happen again."

She looked up at me and smiled gently. "It's okay. I know you love me, and you're working as hard as you can." She rose up onto her knees and hugged me. "Choose joy," she whispered in my ear.

She skipped back to the cottage, and Buddy ran to catch up with her.

I took a deep breath.

She may have been only six, but she always had been fine-tuned to what other people felt.

I loved her. And I loved her confidence in me.

Maybe, just maybe, I could do this.

"Zander, we're out of jerky," Kate called through the open door that night.

"I'll get some more." I leaned the ax against the woodpile I'd been chopping. Glancing at the uneven stack of logs, I felt a pang of embarrassment at my jagged cuts. Pa's firewood never looked that bad.

I walked to the storehouse which held our shrinking supply of preserved food for the colder months. Unfortunately, Pa hadn't had time to can the last batch of the harvest before he died, and I didn't have any idea how to can food myself. So, Kate and I had been eating vegetables constantly these past few days, trying to finish them off before they rotted. The apple trees' limbs hung low, heavy with fruit that would be ready to pick in a couple of weeks. Then, instead of vegetables, we'd be eating mostly apples.

Buddy panted hard when he caught up to me at the storehouse. Before opening the door, my eyes drifted to the charred ruins of the barn in the distance. Only one wall remained standing, and it leaned like an old man. The single black empty window looked like an entrance to a tomb.

No one had seen the smoke, so no one had come to check on us. I guess that's what happens when you live isolated from others. Our farm was tucked away, surrounded by mountains and a huge forest with tall trees. There was also a ring of prickly bushes around the outside of the forest. My family had created the privacy we needed, but it came at a cost. We were very much on our own out here.

I had forbidden Kate from going near what remained of the barn. I'd told her it was because of the broken glass on the ground, but it was really because I was afraid of what she might find. I had gone there as soon as we put the fire out, stepping carefully while calling out for Pa and Drake. It was such a jumbled mess of blackened wood and ash and water that I couldn't even tell where the horse stalls had been or where Drake had rested. I had desperately searched for a survivor, whether human or creature, but when a part of a wall and roof fell, nearly landing on me, I realized that I was no good to Kate dead or injured. As much as I hated to, I had to accept that no one could have survived that fire.

I took a deep breath and tried to clear my mind of the sad thoughts. I gave Buddy a good scratching between his ears. His eyes closed in appreciation as he enjoyed the attention. Just as I reached to lift the latch on the storehouse door, Buddy barked. I jumped at the sudden sound. It was his playful bark. I knew what that used to mean. I shook my head. It couldn't mean that. Buddy's tail wagged, and he panted excitedly.

"No, Buddy, he's gone," I said sadly.

Buddy continued wagging his tail while looking across the field toward the edge of the woods.

Wait, he couldn't have survived the fire. Could he?

I followed Buddy's gaze to the forest, and there stood Drake, all six feet of him, head to toe…or, actually, head to claw. His white belly sparkled in the morning sun, and his green tail stretched out on the ground behind him. He was thinner now, and the bandage on his hind foot was gone.

My mind had wrestled with so many feelings about Drake these past two weeks, mostly anger for the fire he must have started—the fire that killed Pa. I had looked for Drake in the forest a couple of times after the fire, just in case he had managed to escape. After all, we believed dragons to be fireproof. I had checked his favorite sleeping spots but never saw any sign of him, so I assumed the worst—that he'd died in the fire, too. Now here he was, standing at the edge of the forest that circled our property. Seeing the dragon again, right here, alive, made my stomach swirl with conflicting feelings.

Drake plodded toward me, his tail stirring up the fallen leaves as it dragged behind him. Next to me, Buddy dropped his front legs to the ground, his rear sticking up in the air while his wagging tail moved his entire body. He gave a playful growl before sprinting across the field toward his friend. But when Buddy reached Drake, the dragon ignored him and kept walking, his sad eyes looking only at me. Buddy yipped again and ran next to him. When the dragon reached me, Drake looked down at the ground.

I bit my lip, unsure of what to do—unsure of how to act toward him. Part of me was so glad he was alive. And part of me didn't want him to be.

"Drake." My voice wobbled, scratchy and strained. "You're okay after all."

The dragon moaned in response. He blinked, and a tear slid down his snout. Taking a step closer to me, he leaned down and touched his forehead to mine. He moaned again, a mournful sound coming from deep inside him. It contained so much pain and sorrow.

A sob burst from me as the pain I'd been holding forced its way out. My anger toward him eased just a bit. The ache in my throat made it impossible to talk. Instead, I wrapped my arms around his thick neck and bawled. I let it all out. I cried for Pa's death. I cried from all the stress and expectations that now rested on me. I cried in anger toward this dragon who caused the fire. I cried with utter sadness that everything had changed for us in one dark moment.

Drake wrapped his green wings around me, warming me inside and out. We stood like that for a long time. When I couldn't cry anymore, the dragon moaned again.

"I know, Drake," I whispered, my voice trembling. "I'm just going to need some time to get past this."

Tired of waiting on us, Buddy yipped again and jumped onto my leg, pushing me off balance. Our hug ended, and I wiped my face with my sleeve. I rubbed the dog's head. "You're glad to see him, aren't you, boy?"

Buddy barked to get Drake's attention before running across the field. He paused halfway and turned, crouching down with his rear in the air again. He yipped, his tail wagging.

Drake turned to look at me and tilted his head to the side, as if asking permission.

I nodded. "Get him," I encouraged, and Drake dropped to all fours and loped toward the dog. I couldn't hold back a grin.

When Drake caught up to his friend, he rolled over onto his back. Buddy licked the dragon's face with sheer joy as the dragon let out a guttural sound, his legs pumping in the air. Once the greeting was complete, they played chase. Buddy held back his pace as if taunting his slower, bigger friend. I chuckled as I watched them play together.

Drake had been an honorary member of our family for decades. In the early days, he was only half as big as he is now, according to the stories Pa told. His wing was hurt while bravely fighting a bear to save my great-great-grandpa, and he couldn't fly high after that. Pa always thought that was why Drake had never flown away.

But in my heart, I liked to think the dragon just loved us too much to leave.

There stood Drake, all six feet of him.

Chapter 3

Red, orange, and yellow leaves twirled in chilly breezes as the days grew shorter. Our days turned into weeks, and before I realized it, a month had passed since the fire.

Kate and I had fallen into a comfortable routine. I worked on repairs and projects as I could, feeling especially proud of myself when I finally fixed the handle to the well. I had endured blisters and sweat-stiffened clothes, but I'd finished it and installed it. And it worked! Each success made me feel a little more confident in my ability to take care of Kate and our home. She helped me when she could and had become a "little momma" to me after my hammer-throwing meltdown.

"Zander?" Kate's eyes said it all. She wanted something. "It's getting colder outside."

I nodded but said nothing as I sliced apples for part of our dinner.

"Um..." She wrung her hands together and bit her lip before saying, "You know Drake doesn't like sleeping outside in the cold. And since the barn burned down...," she shrugged.

When she didn't continue, I finished the request for her. "You want him to sleep in the storehouse?"

She giggled. "No, silly. It's too small." She paused and answered more softly, "I want him to sleep...here." She pointed to the floor.

"Here?"

She nodded. "Here. In the house. With us." I raised my eyebrows and waited, so she hurriedly continued. "You've been training him. He knows commands just like Buddy. He would behave. I know he would." She waited for a moment and then gave me a pouty face. "Please?"

It was true that I'd been training Drake. At first, I had trained Buddy with typical dog commands. After some of my training sessions in the field with Buddy, I'd noticed Drake watching from a distance. A few sessions later, Drake came closer until I sensed a hint of understanding. I gave the "sit" command to Buddy, and Drake sat, too. That's when I decided to train both of them. It didn't take long for them to turn it into a competition, seeing who could master the new skill first. If Buddy succeeded first, he showed his pride by turning tight circles and yipping, but Drake would celebrate by raising his head and letting out a short burst of fire.

I sighed, realizing Kate was right; Drake did hate the cold. Pa's voice rumbled through my head, reminding me that we owed it to the dragon. So, without saying a thing, I went outside. Kate squealed when Buddy and I came in, followed by a very hesitant Drake. He ducked his head beneath the door frame as he walked on his hind legs.

"This is a trial run, just for tonight," I told her, "so don't get your hopes up."

Kate laughed and clapped excitedly.

I already regretted the idea.

The dragon stood in the doorway, looking all around. He'd never been inside the cottage. Seeing it through Drake's eyes,

I realized it must look tiny compared to the big barn where he used to sleep during cold weather. Our living room had some wooden chairs and a small side table in front of the fireplace. The eating table and its chairs stood near the wall, and the kitchen workspace was in the corner. Two doors on either side of the fireplace led to bedrooms. One had been Pa's, and Kate and I shared the other one. I'd never found the courage to claim Pa's bedroom for myself after the fire. Besides, Kate sometimes woke up with nightmares and needed me to calm her down.

Kate moved the furniture away from the fireplace, gathered some quilts, and made a wide mound that looked a lot like the nest Drake had used in the barn. I didn't have first-hand knowledge of other dragons' habits, but I knew warmth was very important to this one.

Drake immediately went to work arranging it to his satisfaction. Before he settled into it, he lightly blew fire on the logs inside the cold hearth, and orange and yellow flames sprung to life. The dragon curled into a ball, his snout tucked down among the quilts, and the room soon filled with the sound of steady, deep breathing. A nap had begun.

Kate and I worked together to prepare a meal of cheese, sliced apples, cured meat, and bread. We sat at the table to eat, and, out of habit, she tossed Buddy a small piece of cheese from her plate. I cringed as soon as the cheese left her hand. Buddy always chewed noisily, and this time, the noise woke Drake. The dragon lifted his head and watched Buddy with rapt attention before jumping up to sit next to the dog.

Kate giggled when she saw them sitting side by side. Drake looked just like a dog begging for food—but much, much taller...and greener.

"Watch this!" she said. Before I could stop her, she threw a piece of cheese to Drake. Her aim was off, though, and it sailed over his head and landed behind him.

Not one to miss a food hand-out, Buddy immediately jumped up, and the race was on. Drake's long tail knocked into the table as he turned, and our tin plates slid to the floor with a clang. Kate squealed while I sat there with my mouth hanging open. Buddy was the quicker of the two and gobbled up our fallen food, not even bothering to chew it.

After finding his little piece of wayward cheese, Drake looked over his shoulder at Buddy who sat next to the overturned plates. The dog's tongue lazily cleaned his snout. The dragon took a step toward Buddy, but I jumped between them with outstretched arms. I had to end this immediately.

"No!" I called out to both of them, my voice as stern and Pa-like as I could make it. "Buddy, Drake, outside!" Buddy knew the command, so he immediately walked to the door. Drake went back to his fireside nest and had just gotten comfortable when I stood at the door and called a drawn out, "Nooo," which caught the dragon's attention. When he saw me shoo Buddy outside, he looked at Kate with sad eyes, as if hoping she could change my mind.

She shook her head. "No. Outside, Drake," she said softly, pointing to the open door.

With his head drooping and his tail dragging across the floor, Drake went outside. Oh, he looked so pitiful. If I weren't so mad about the wasted food, I might have found it funny.

As Kate picked up the plates from the floor, she asked, "We can give Drake another chance, right? He's still learning."

"Another chance?" I fought to control my voice as I shut the door. I shook my head. "That's not likely. He's just too big to be inside." I walked to the kitchen.

"But there's nowhere else for him to go when it's cold," she whined, putting the plates in the wash bucket. "And he's family."

I sighed. She was right. Winter was coming. We would have to come up with a plan for him.

"I'll have to think about it." I put the lid on the tin of dried meat, noticing it was almost empty again. We were going through our food too quickly. "And I told you before: stop giving Buddy food from the table. We have to be careful, so we won't run out. It's not like we can go into town, since the horses are...well, you know."

"What? We could run out of food?" She looked at me with her big green eyes. "What will we do then?"

I put an arm around her shoulder and drew her closer to me. "I don't know, but we'll figure it out together, okay?" I gave her a forced smile.

She nodded. She fully trusted me to have everything figured out.

Too bad I didn't.

Two months after the fire, we had eaten through most of our food supply, despite my creative efforts to make it last. I had tried watering down our soups and slicing food into thinner pieces so it looked like we had more on our plates. I doubted we had enough food to make it through the winter. If not for the barn fire, we would've still had our chickens and eggs, and our goat for milk and cheese. Otherwise, we might have been able to make this work.

I considered training Drake to hunt for us. That would take care of our food problem, but Drake's idea of edible meat made me shudder. At least he'd been trained by my grandfather to bury the bones, so we were spared from seeing that.

I thought about going to a neighbor's house to ask for help, but the nearest house was a half-hour's ride, and the horses had died in the fire.

My family had kept to ourselves on purpose. When we moved to the cottage to live with Grandma after Grandpa died, Pa taught me the importance of keeping Drake a secret. Many years ago, Grandpa had planted thorny bushes along the outer edge of the forest that surrounded the farm to keep people away. We knew the easiest way through, but it was well hidden from outsiders. Drake's existence had been kept a secret for decades, and it needed to stay that way. Besides, no one could know that Kate and I were now alone. Terrified we'd be separated or shipped off to the orphanage in Trulith, the nearest kingdom, it had become my mission to do everything I could to keep us hidden and safe.

Kate's days were filled with chores she could handle, like washing our clothes, sweeping the house, and helping me with the meals. But I also made sure she spent plenty of time outdoors playing with Buddy and Drake. I worked on training them when I found the time. I tried my best to repair things that had broken, like Kate's rocking chair, but some were beyond my abilities and now lay hidden out of sight behind the cottage. I fell into bed with aching muscles, exhausted every night.

As we expected for this time of year, the wind picked up and the temperature dropped. The season I'd been dreading was now on its way.

When an early snow came, Kate bundled up and played outside, giggling as she tried to catch the fluffy white flakes. Drake and Buddy joined her, and the sight through the window made me smile. I returned to sit by the fire, allowing myself a little time to relax. I pulled out my whittling project and worked on carving a horse. The shavings went into the bucket between my feet. Pa had taught me to whittle, and each time I did it, I felt like he was there with me.

Kate opened the door to come inside. Buddy ran in just before she pushed the door closed against the bitterly cold wind trying to fight its way into the cottage. The dog shook his furry body from head to toe, dotting the wooden floor with water drops. Then he came to lay near me in front of the fire.

"It's so cold out there!" Kate said, her cheeks rosy red. A few snowflakes lay in her hair poking out beneath her knitted cap. After hanging her coat and cap, she sat next to me and held out her hands to be warmed by the fire.

"Zander?" she asked meekly. Her voice told me she was about to ask for something I wouldn't like. "Um, since it's so cold outside…and with the snow falling…" She paused.

Oh no. I knew what was coming. "Just say it, Kate."

"Well, I was just thinking that maybe Drake could sleep inside tonight."

I gave her a pointed look.

She nodded and raised her eyebrows, a slight smile on her lips. I scowled, irritated. Her smile faded, and she stared into the fire. "You know how he doesn't like the cold. And he doesn't have the barn to stay in now."

"But Drake—"

"I know what happened the last time he came in," she interrupted, "but that was my fault."

"Yeah, he got too excited, knocked over furniture, and Buddy ate our food. And now you want Drake to stay in here all night long?"

She turned, her eyes pleading for me to understand. "You've taught him the command to stay. We could make him stay in front of the fireplace and not get up until we tell him to. Then he won't be able to knock anything over."

I said nothing for a moment as I considered my options, like Pa had taught me to do when I wasn't sure about a decision. If I didn't agree to this, Kate would be unbearable to live with. And she was right, Drake hated the cold, and he knew the stay command. Sometimes, I believed the dragon was a better trained dog than Buddy.

"All right, we'll let him in tonight but only on a trial basis." I had barely said the words before Kate jumped up and hugged me. Those were basically the same words I'd said before. I hoped for a better outcome this time.

"Oh, thank you, thank you!" She ran toward the door. "I'm going to get Drake right now!" She lifted her coat from the peg and opened the door.

As it turned out, she didn't need her coat after all. There, in front of her, on all fours was Drake, his head down and shoulders hunched.

"Here you are!" she squealed. "Come inside, Drake," she called, motioning with her hand. "Come in and get warm."

The dragon stepped hesitantly into the cottage, looking at me for permission.

"What, am I your keeper?" I scoffed at him just standing there.

Blink, blink, blink was Drake's response.

"Huh, yeah, I guess I am." I rolled my eyes but couldn't stifle a chuckle at how pitiful he looked. "Come in, big guy, but you'd better behave."

Once his tail dragged all the way in, Kate closed the door. Buddy yipped and wagged his tail as he greeted his friend. Drake leaned down and nuzzled the dog's fur.

I moved the chairs against the wall to make room for our overnight guest, and Kate again covered the floor in front of the fireplace with quilts. I motioned for Drake to lie down, and he immediately obeyed. His green scales shimmered in the firelight. Once Drake was situated, Buddy curled up next to him, their bodies touching, scale to fur.

If only I'd said no to Kate, things would have turned out quite differently.

Chapter 4

Thankfully, the early snow was short-lived. The snow melted, but a chill remained in the air. Drake spent the days outside, and Buddy usually tagged along. I often wondered about the adventures they had together. Then at nightfall, they both returned, immediately falling asleep, side-by-side, in front of the fire. Buddy was happy to have someone to snuggle with, and Drake seemed content to have a warm place to sleep.

One morning, a noise woke me from a deep sleep. I stared at the ceiling as I listened, warm and cozy under Ma's quilts. The early morning sunrise streamed in through the curtains, filling the bedroom with a strange shade of orange.

There! I heard it again—a quiet moan, like a growl but with a ticking or bubbling sound. It came from the other room. I hardly breathed as my imagination ran through all sorts of possibilities. Then I heard a shuffle, and the noise stopped.

That's when I realized what it was: Drake. Just as Buddy sometimes ran in his sleep, Drake was prone to nightmares and snoring. The first time it happened, I had been whittling near the two sleeping friends, and Buddy scooted close against Drake, waking him up just enough to make him stop moaning and return to sleep.

Now that I knew what the sound was, I let out a breath in relief. I waited to hear the noise again, but it never came. Rolling over, I tried to go back to sleep, but after tossing and turning for a while, I decided I might as well start on my chores for the day. I got dressed, being careful not to wake Kate. If she woke up too early, I'd have to endure her endless whining and grumpiness until she decided she was ready to act like a decent human being.

Drake and Buddy lay cuddled up against each other in front of the dying fire. Normally, I started these chilly mornings by stirring the embers and adding a few more logs to the fire. But the two were sleeping so soundly, I decided to leave well enough alone and tend to the fire when I returned.

Moving quietly, I shrugged into my coat and wrapped a scarf around my neck. I placed one of Pa's old wide-brimmed hats on my head as I kept an eye on the sleepers. After removing the ax that hung on the wall, I braced myself against the bitter wind as I hurried out the door. I closed it quietly, hoping not to wake anyone inside. I pulled the scarf up over my mouth and ducked my head, burying my chin into my coat as I hurried across the open field to the woods.

I always enjoyed being in the forest. It felt like being with Pa again as memories came to mind of chopping wood with him. A twinge of sadness threatened to overtake my happy thoughts, so I shook them away. I had too much to do to allow myself bad feelings that would only slow me down.

As the sun gradually made its way into the sky, I shoved my scarf into my coat pocket, glad of the slight warmth filling the air. The wind continued, though, and I retrieved my hat from its grip a few times before I anchored it to the ground with a piece of wood. About the time I decided I had enough firewood for the next several days, my stomach rumbled, reminding me that I hadn't eaten breakfast. Gathering as much wood as I could carry on this first trip, I walked toward the open field. I missed having the pull-cart Pa used for taking the logs to the cottage. The cart had been stored in the barn and went up in flames with everything else.

Passing the last tree in the woods, I glanced up at the sky, a beautiful blue with only a few wispy clouds. Other than the wind, it looked like it would be a nice day.

Then I saw it.

Smoke.

Coming from the cottage!

Kate screamed my name. I threw the firewood to the ground and ran, unaware I still held the ax in my hand.

Smoke rose through the front window with the occasional lick of an orange-red flame. My feet couldn't carry me fast enough.

"Kate!"

I reached the front door of the cottage, the only door, and felt the heat from the flames. If I opened that door, the flames would grow worse.

Kate screamed for me again.

I stifled a sob. I had to get inside!

I ran around to the back window. "Kate?" I screamed, banging on the window with my open hand.

"Zander!"

"I'm here! Back away from the window!" I waited only a moment before I smashed the glass with the ax. Smoke billowed out of its new escape route. I heard Kate cough. Using the ax like a hammer, I cleared the remaining glass along the window frame. I dropped it and climbed inside.

Smoke filled the entire house. My eyes burned, making it hard to see. My lungs begged for clean air. I pulled the scarf out of my pocket and quickly wrapped it around my head, covering my mouth and nose.

I plunged into the smoke, heading in the direction of her cough.

"Kate!" My lungs burned just as I felt her arms around me. I carried her to the window and lifted her through it. "Get a bucket of water and pass it to me through here. Hurry!"

The smoke was so thick, I had to feel my way across the room. I found the nearby pitchers and wash basins and emptied them on the fire which now lapped at the front door. Kate brought a full bucket, struggling to lift it to the window. I pulled it inside, threw the water at the base of the flames, and returned the bucket to Kate.

"Another!" I shouted as I rubbed my stinging eyes. I coughed, sticking my head out the window as I gasped for fresh air.

I lost count of the number of buckets of water it took before the flames finally died. My eyes stung so badly, I could hardly keep them open. I tried to open the front door for fresh air, but it wouldn't budge. I kicked at the half-burned wood, and the door creaked mournfully as it fell outward, along with a large part of the wall. It landed with a thud. We now had a huge, open view of the forest.

Great.

I stepped outside and coughed, a deep raspy sound coming from me. My lungs burned with each breath. The fresh air couldn't get into them fast enough.

"Kate!" I called between coughs.

She ran around the corner of the house and hugged me tightly.

"Are you okay?" I asked, pulling her away so I could look at her.

Two clear lines ran down her cheeks where tears had washed through the soot. She gasped. "Buddy! Drake!"

She let go of me and ran back into the cottage. I was right behind her, ready to shield her from what she might find. We waved the smoke away from our faces. In our bedroom, we found Drake facing the corner, crouched into a ball.

I opened the window to release the remaining smoke.

"Where's Buddy?" Kate asked as a sick feeling stopped my breath. "Buddy?" she called sweetly, although there was no mistaking the tinge of panic in her voice.

A quiet whine sounded, and Kate crouched down on the floor next to my bed. She lifted the quilt, and Buddy crawled out, his white fur tinted gray from the smoke.

"Oh, Buddy! Are you okay?" She hugged him and checked him over. "He doesn't look hurt."

Buddy walked to Drake and barked at him. The dragon turned around sheepishly, his eyes on the floor.

It only took me a moment to piece it together. "A nightmare," I growled, pointing to Drake as I turned to Kate. "He did this. He must have breathed fire during a bad dream." I had to tamp down the anger boiling inside of me. "Buddy, Drake, outside!" I yelled, pointing to what used to be the door. They walked past me, Drake's head hanging low.

"He didn't mean to do it," Kate pleaded. "You can tell he's sorry."

"Sorry?" I stomped into the main room, and my foot went through the floor. "Take a look around you!"

She peeked through the doorway and saw what I saw. What remained of the chairs and table lay haphazardly in pieces. The floor was charred and now had a foot-sized hole in it. Most of the front wall and the entire door were missing.

I spread my arms out. "He destroyed our house, Kate!" My voice shook in anger mixed with fear. "Winter's almost here, and I can't possibly fix this!"

A cold wind pushed its way through the missing wall, proving my point.

"Oh, Zander," Kate said softly as she looked around. She grabbed my hand and held on tight.

We were homeless.

Chapter 5

"Zander, I'm cold," Kate whined for the forty-seventh time.

We'd been walking for days. I had tried to make our journey sound like an exciting adventure. For the first two days, Kate liked the idea of sleeping under the stars and traveling in search of new places, but eventually she'd caught on and realized it wasn't nearly as fun as I had made it sound.

Now, I closed my eyes and inhaled sharply, pushing away the negative words that lingered on the tip of my tongue. They would only make her cry.

"I know, Kate. I'm cold, too."

Choose joy. Choose joy. Choose joy.

Ma had told me stories about attending the king's coronation when she was a little girl living in the beautiful kingdom of Trulith. That's where we were headed. She'd said a huge forest lay to the east of it, and the forest was so large, it would take a full day to walk through it. I thought it might serve as a hidden home for Drake. He was used to the woods around our property back home, so I hoped this would work for him.

I'm sure we were an odd sight—a boy with a pack on his back and his father's overly large sword hanging from his belt; a little girl with a smaller pack on her back and a doll held tightly in her arm; a white dog with a curly tail happily leaping through fields and chasing butterflies and grasshoppers...and a huge green dragon walking on all fours, carrying evenly-weighted packs on each side that were held in place with belts and rope.

Staying unseen remained constantly at the front of my mind as we walked. We avoided roadways and worn paths, usually walking single file under cover of the trees or through tall fields. Anytime Buddy or Drake sensed danger, we darted into a grove of trees or lay low in a field to hide.

Once, when we thought someone was coming, Drake hid himself by standing upright behind a big tree. Despite the width of the tree trunk, Drake was much wider, so his belly stuck out from one side of the tree, and his back with our packs stuck out from the other side. He stood straight as an arrow, though, fully believing his effort to hide was working. It was one of the funniest things I'd ever seen. I struggled to keep my snickers quiet until we heard the clomp of hooves pass by in the distance. When Kate called Drake to come out, he poked his head around the tree trunk, eyes wide, totally unaware that he'd completely failed at hiding himself. Kate and I laughed about that for a long time.

"When can we stop?" Kate whined behind me. "My feet hurt, and my doll is tired."

She had removed her pack and now dragged it on the ground. With her hair in her face and her shoulders sagging, she was definitely done.

I stopped and waited for her to catch up to me. I put my arm around her shoulder, pulling her close to my side. "I'm sure your doll's tired. She's traveled a long way, hasn't she?" Kate nodded as her lower lip quivered. "And I know you're tired, too. I'll tell you what—let's focus on a point where we'll walk to, like a goal. And when we reach that goal, we'll decide if we can make it to another goal or if we need to stop for the day. Can you do that?"

She sniffed and looked up at me, her eyes filled with unshed tears. "I can try."

I gave her a reassuring smile and pointed at a grove of trees far in the distance. "Do you see those trees up ahead?" I asked. She nodded. "Let's aim for those, and we'll decide about whether to stop once we reach them. That'll be our first goal."

"Okay," she said and took a big wobbly breath. She hugged her doll to her chest.

I carried her pack for her as we walked silently. Instead of walking ahead, I stayed beside her, on alert for signs of a meltdown. After a while, Kate began to hum, and I recognized the tune.

"Ma used to sing that to us," I said. "You remember it?"

"Uh huh."

"She sang that when you cried. She held you in her arms and swayed back and forth, and it was like magic how it quieted you so fast. You must have loved that song."

I listened as she started the tune again. Kate put her doll up on her shoulder and patted its back as if to calm it.

Before she complained again, we reached our goal—the grove of trees that had once seemed so far away.

"We did it!" she said.

"Yes, we did. That wasn't so hard, was it?" She shook her head, and I kept talking to keep the mood light. "So, what do you think, traveling girl? Can you go further?" I looked ahead and saw a tall wooden building that looked like it had been abandoned long ago. "If you think you can make it to that shack up ahead, maybe we can sleep in there tonight."

"And not sleep under the stars?" She sounded a little disappointed.

"Well, if you want to sleep under the stars, I guess we can. But the nights are getting colder, and I think Buddy's ready to sleep inside for a change. I think he might be missing our house."

"I miss it, too," she said wistfully. "What about Drake? Can he sleep inside with us?"

I frowned. "He's not good inside a house. We already know that."

"He might do better now, since he'll be tired from all this walking. Maybe he'll go right to sleep." I didn't respond. "You can't stay mad at him forever," she whispered.

I shook my head in frustration and tried to keep my voice steady. "I'm not sure we can trust him. Just so you know, I've been wondering if maybe he should be out on his own, out in the wild. He *is* a dragon, after all."

We'd had this same discussion before we left our charred cottage. My anger wanted to punish the dragon and shoo him away from us, but Kate wouldn't let me. She reminded me that Drake was family, and family looks out for each other and loves each other, no matter what bad things we might do. Kate was often a better person than I was.

"But he's not a regular dragon," she insisted. "He's family, and he loves us. Papa said so." She took my hand and squeezed it. "And if Drake starts to have a bad dream, I can wake him up."

I just sighed.

Kate hadn't noticed that we'd kept walking and were making steady progress toward the shack. She let out a yawn. Behind us, Drake yawned, too.

As we neared the shack, I noticed that the whole building leaned to the right. Dark, empty rectangles stood where windows once had been. Wooden planks hung loosely from the sides like broken limbs. I made Kate wait at a distance while I checked inside. Dirt scraped under my feet as I walked into the small space. Dried crumpled leaves littered the wooden floor. Cobwebs hung in the rafters, and the smell of dust and rot lingered in the air. The roof looked solid, though, with only bits of the fading sunlight streaming through.

I took off my pack and set it against the wall before poking my head outside. I smiled. "Come on in."

Buddy bounded into the shabby building, went to a corner, and curled up in a ball.

Kate came to the door and peered inside. "It'll be okay for us to sleep in here tonight?" she asked timidly.

"It's sturdy enough, and we'll have a roof over our heads. Well," I looked up, "most of a roof. It should work fine."

She took a few steps inside and was nearly knocked off her feet by Drake who had come up behind her. I put both of my hands out to slow the excited dragon.

"Woah, Drake. Be careful. Easy," I said, scowling.

The dragon came inside more slowly. Buddy lifted his sleepy head to see what was going on, but he quickly lost interest and closed his eyes again.

I signaled for Drake to turn around, and I took the large packs off his back. He stood on his hind legs and stretched while I closed the squeaky door. After looking around the one-room building, Drake reached out with the gentlest of motions and picked up Kate. She squealed with surprise as he lifted her to his chest before carefully curling up on the floor, cradling Kate in his arms.

Kate giggled softly. "Zander, did you see?"

Just when I thought I'd seen every possible human-like behavior from Drake, the dragon surprised me with something new. "It looks like Drake's going to take care of you tonight."

As the chilly night air whispered through the cracks of the old shack, I set aside my uncertainty and curled up beside his warm body, instantly falling asleep.

Chapter 6

Houses began to pop up more and more often, like daisies in springtime. We managed to stay out of sight of anyone traveling near us, but I had a nagging feeling in my gut that we were definitely getting close to a town.

Around midday, we came across another abandoned house. This one was much bigger than the shack we'd slept in the night before. Instead of being run down, though, this house had been damaged by a bad fire. Part of the roof and the upper half of a wall were missing. Tattered curtains fluttered through openings where once were windows. I had never been inside a house so large, and I felt an itch to wander through it. I wondered if this was the size of house Ma had grown up in. Pa used to joke with Ma about her knowing how the "other half" lived because of her upbringing in Trulith. She always assured him that love was more important than any "things" she could own.

My traveling group and I knelt behind some large boulders not far from the ruined house.

"What are we doing?" Kate asked in an exaggerated whisper.

"*You* are going to stay here with Buddy and Drake. *I* am going to check out that house and make sure no one's inside."

She pulled on my arm. "Don't leave us alone," she whined.

I carefully pried her fingers from their grip. "It'll be fine. It looks empty, but I need to make sure. Maybe we can rest inside for a little while before we keep walking."

She twirled her finger in her hair, then nodded. "Okay, but hurry, please."

I gave Drake and Buddy the stay command, left my pack with Kate, and crouched low as I ran through the tall grass toward the house. I paused for a moment when I spotted two wooden crosses marking graves now partly hidden by intrusive weeds. Beyond that were the remains of a garden strangled with a jungle of twisted vines and wildflowers.

I leaned against an outer wall, stopping beneath one of the broken windows, and I slowly raised myself enough to peek inside. It was a bedroom with a child's empty bed frame and a dust-covered dresser with its drawers hanging open. Leaves and twigs littered the floor. Whoever lived here had left with no intention of coming back.

Tiptoeing around to the front of the house, I opened the door, wincing as it creaked hauntingly. Standing motionless, I listened and watched for any sign of life. I took a deep breath for courage and walked inside. The familiar smell of smoke mingled in the breeze that followed me in.

To the left was a dining room with a table and four chairs, and on the wall above was a faded painting slowly freeing itself from its fancy wooden frame. Just beyond an open doorway, I caught a glimpse of a small kitchen. To my right was a sitting area with a padded chair and couch. I had never seen either before, but I remembered that Ma and Pa had hoped to get padded furniture one day to replace our wooden chairs. I couldn't wait to show them to Kate.

"Hello?" I called, hoping upon hope that no one was there. I took a few more steps inside. "Hello?"

The only sounds were the creaking floorboards and the wind whistling through broken windows.

I peered outside the door to make sure the coast was clear before I ran to Kate's hiding spot. She heard me coming and popped up from behind the boulder.

"Well?" she asked with a hopeful look on her face. When she saw my smile, she clapped excitedly. "Yay! Let's go!"

I grabbed my pack and waved for them to follow me. Buddy reached the house first and immediately began sniffing around.

Once inside, I watched Kate's reaction when she saw the couch and chair. I laughed at her astonishment.

"What is this?" she asked. She walked to the dirty, padded couch and ran her hands along it. She pushed down on the seat and gasped when it popped back up. "It's smushy!" She turned to look at me. "Can I?"

"Of course! Make yourself comfortable, my good lady." I waved my arm with a flourish.

"Thank you, sir," she giggled.

When we both plopped down, surprise washed over us. It was like sinking into a cloud compared to our hard wooden chairs at home.

A thumping sound near the front door made me jump. Drake stood upright in the doorway. He took a step, but his packs thumped against the wood, stopping him from going any further. He turned and stepped forward, but again, the packs thumped against the doorway. Drake looked at me with sad eyes and whimpered.

Chuckling, I walked to him. "I think your bundles are too big."

After telling him to get down on all fours, I unbuckled the packs and dragged them inside. "Okay, now come in."

Drake stood and poked his head through the open doorway, unsure of whether to try again. Kate giggled and waved for him to come inside. He ducked his head and passed through the opening without a problem. Buddy ran to him and yipped in celebration before rushing off down the hallway. Drake followed.

I moved our packs to the couch. "We need to go through our stuff. I think there's a town coming up. I can try to sell some things to get us money so I can buy what we need."

"Like more food?"

"Tired of the jerky?" I asked with a pretend look of shock.

She snickered in response.

"Yes, like food," I answered. "And some warmer clothes for our travels." With us only being able to take what we could carry in our packs, I'd had to decide what was most important to bring. Obviously, I was no expert at this.

"First, can we explore the rest of the house?" Kate folded her hands beneath her chin as if saying a prayer. "Please? I've never been in a house this big or this fancy."

I smiled, eager to check it out, too. She cheered and grabbed my hand to pull me off the couch before leading me down the hallway.

To the right was the open door to the bedroom I'd seen through the window. Kate went into it, holding her doll in her arm, while I walked ahead to see where Buddy and Drake had gone.

The room across the hall was missing most of the roof as well as part of the wall. When I reached the room at the end of the hallway, I found Drake and Buddy eagerly investigating. This bedroom had the most fire damage. The roof was completely gone. The large bed's straw mattress was mostly burned. The room also held the charred remains of a desk and chair and two other pieces of furniture burned beyond recognition. This must have been the parents' bedroom.

Buddy wagged his tail at me before leaving the room to explore elsewhere, but Drake stood near one of the burned walls, sniffing intently. At first, I thought he might be crying, but he held his snout close to the wall and continued sniffing as he walked. No, the dragon had caught the scent of something.

"What is it, Drake?" I asked, coming up behind him.

He jumped when I spoke. He'd been so focused, he hadn't heard me approach. Drake turned toward me, confusion in his eyes. He looked back at the wall and then at the burned damage in the room before looking at me again.

Footsteps stopped in the doorway. "Is this where the fire started?" Kate whispered, shocked at the destruction.

"Maybe. I'm guessing the family couldn't fix the house, so they took what they could and left." I certainly wasn't going to tell her about the graves I'd seen outside. I shoved my hands in my pockets, not wanting to dwell on this anymore. "Hey, let's go through our stuff. Then we can rest for a while before we hit the road again."

Kate and I sat on the couch and emptied our packs. Before we'd left home, I had looked through what hadn't burned and took what I thought I could sell. If we could get coin for our items, we could buy additional food and other things we needed. Then eventually, hopefully, we would make it to Trulith and find a new place to live—somewhere Drake would be safe, and I could get a job to provide what Kate and I needed.

As we made a pile of the things to sell, nearly every item brought a warm memory of my parents. The candlesticks reminded me of Pa reading his favorite books aloud by candlelight with Kate and me sitting on the floor near his feet. A small can of buttons had belonged to Ma, and I pictured her mending clothes by the light from the fireplace.

"Do you remember this?" I lifted a small frying pan.

"That hung on the kitchen wall."

"Yeah, but can you think of a time when it was actually used for cooking?"

Kate scrunched her face in thought. "No, I don't remember, but I'm kind of little, and my brain has a lot of thoughts."

Caught off-guard by her comment, I snorted as I laughed out loud.

She smiled and pointed at me. "You sounded like a pig!"

My cheeks grew warm, but my grin remained. I grabbed her pointing finger playfully. "You are a funny girl. Do you know that?" I turned the pan around in my hand. "Pa was funny like that, too. One time, before Ma got sick, they were making dinner together, joking around like they always did. I don't remember what they were talking about, but I remember that she was getting sassy. Next thing we knew, Pa pulled this pan out of the cabinet and smacked Ma's bottom with it."

Kate covered her mouth as she laughed.

"Not hard, just playfully," I said. "They both laughed until they had tears coming out of their eyes, and then they hugged, still laughing." I smiled at the memory, and my heart felt lighter. "After Ma died, Pa hung the pan on the wall and said he wanted it to remind him of that silly moment and how much they loved each other."

"I wish I could remember that." Kate pulled out a framed drawing. "Oh, we can't sell this, Zander," she said with a frown.

It was a charcoal drawing of a beautiful castle set on a hill with mountains in the background. Ma drew it long before I was born. Pa always said she had the talent of a true artist. The drawing was of Trulith, where Ma had lived when she was little—the place I longed to see with my own eyes. I used to stare at that picture as it hung on the wall of our home, imagining how grand life must be there.

I gently took the drawing from Kate's hand and put it in the pack we filled with the things to keep. "You're right. We'll never sell this one."

Later, while Kate napped on the couch, Buddy and Drake rested side-by-side on the floor. I repacked our bags, filling mine with items to sell at the next town. I had never tried to sell anything before. The few times we'd gone into a town with Pa, he and Ma did all the talking. The thought of tomorrow's task weighed heavily on my heart, making it feel like there was a lump in my chest that would never go away.

Chapter 7

The next day, we saw a few small houses scattered along the side of a tall, wide hill. As we climbed the hill, we made sure to stay out of sight of the buildings. Reaching the top, we saw a small town in the valley below. We ducked out of sight behind a group of tall, thick bushes while I stood and peered carefully over the top to study the layout. Buddy and Drake eagerly lay down beside us.

Kate stuck her head out from her hiding place and frowned. "That doesn't look like Ma's picture of Trulith. There's not even a castle."

I gently pulled her down to sit next to me. "No, silly, that's not Trulith. You'll know it when we get there. The town down there is where I'm going to sell some of our stuff, like we talked about earlier."

"You keep saying *you're* going to sell them, but what about me?"

I put on a serious face and shook my head. "I don't think I'd get much for you. I'm not even going to try to sell you."

She gasped and her eyes grew wide, then she scowled and elbowed me, hard enough to make it hurt. She laughed at my pain.

"All right, all right." I rubbed my ribs. "Actually, I'm worried about the two of us being seen wandering the streets without a grown-up. The last thing we need is to have someone questioning us."

Kate's shoulders slumped. "I can't go with you? I have to stay here by myself?"

"You won't be by yourself. Buddy and Drake are here, and they need you to stay so they won't think we've left them." I peered around the bush and pointed to a large group of trees curving around one side of the town "I've got it figured out. I'll walk you down there, and you three can wait in those woods while I'm gone. We're lucky this town is bordered by a forest, so you'll have a safe hiding place while you wait. I'll meet you there as soon as I'm done."

Leaving them alone filled me with worry, since only one of the three could understand what I was saying, and she was only six. But I just couldn't risk her coming with me or leaving Drake by himself.

Once we reached the woods and found a place far enough inside that felt safe, I heaved my pack onto my shoulders and gave Kate a big hug.

"Be careful," she said, her voice quivering as she twirled a strand of hair around her finger.

I gently pushed her hand down to her side and gave her fingers a light squeeze. "Always," I said softly. I tucked the twirled strand of hair behind her ear. "Remember, I'll come right back here as soon as I'm done. Make sure Drake stays out of sight." She nodded. "The next time you see me, I'll have some food for us."

She smiled at that. We hadn't eaten much the last two days, trying to conserve what little food remained. I felt constantly hungry. I was sure she did, too.

Before I left, I gave Buddy a good head-scratching and chuckled when the dog closed his eyes and sighed with pleasure.

"Take care of them," I said to Drake, doubting he understood but hoping, nonetheless. "Be good." Then I turned to the dog and dragon and held up my hand. "Stay," I said.

Drake glanced at Buddy, then at Kate, and then at me. His eyes held confusion and concern, as if he understood that I was leaving them. I gave him what I hoped was a reassuring smile.

The thought of leaving them behind twisted my stomach into knots. So much could go wrong while I was gone. I had to hurry. Hitching my pack higher up on my back, I took a deep breath and hustled down the main road that led into town.

Wooden walkways stretched out like bridges between colorless buildings. Grown-ups bustled in and out of shops along the cobblestone street, while wide gaps between some stores opened up into dirt paths that led to another street beyond.

I walked into a small general store, noticing a few customers shopping inside. I stopped at the sales counter just inside the door. The air smelled of cinnamon. Sunlight filtered in through the windows, giving me a brightened view of the colorful fabrics and candy jars along the back wall, as well as a nearby table of lanterns and tools. A woman stood behind the counter, her gray hair gathered in a loose bun on top of her head. She gave me a warm smile which immediately put me at ease.

"What can I do for you, young man?" she asked, placing her forearms on the counter as she leaned toward me.

My voice cracked as I began to speak. Clearing my throat, I tried again. "Uh, I have a few things I need to sell, and I was wondering if you might be interested in them."

The saleswoman raised her eyebrows in interest, so I removed my pack. I pulled out two candlesticks and an empty oil lamp and placed them on the counter. She picked up each one and inspected it carefully while I dug in my pack and pulled out Ma's button box, a spool of ribbon, and a few other things.

The woman narrowed her eyes slightly. "You didn't steal these, did you?"

"N—no, ma'am. They belonged to my homestead but...but my parents don't need them anymore. We need food instead."

Her face relaxed. She pushed the items over to the side and gave a quick look around the store before leaning toward me. "You seem like an honest young man. There are several families around here who've fallen on hard times, so I understand that. I do. Tell you what...I can't pay you in coin for these, but I can exchange them for other items. Go pick what you need, and I'll let you know if that's enough to settle our exchange. Okay?"

I smiled as relief washed through me. "Yes, ma'am. Thank you."

After I put the now-lighter pack onto my shoulder, she handed me a woven basket from behind the counter. Glancing around the store, I quickly found the food section and thought very carefully as I selected each item, mostly looking for things we could eat as we walked. In the basket, I put two loaves of bread and a jar of jam, as well as a large chunk of hard cheese wrapped in a cloth. An open barrel of jerky caught my attention. Even though we'd been eating a lot of it since we'd left home and were both kind of sick of it, I had to admit that it did travel well. We could easily eat it as we walked, and Buddy liked jerky, too. Reluctantly, I scooped some into a sack and put it in the basket. I ignored the open bins of flour, corn, and other grains. Instead, I added several apples, oranges, and a bunch of carrots to the basket, hoping Kate would be happy with my choices.

Once I felt like I had gathered enough to equal what I was selling, I returned to the counter. The saleswoman pulled each item from the basket while she jotted notes on her paper.

Finally, the woman sighed lightly. "No, I'm sorry. I just don't think this is going to work."

My heart skipped a beat and then began to pound. My mind raced to consider what I could return to the shelves.

"I see the items you're planning to purchase here," she continued, "but there aren't any treats." She paused and smiled when my concerned eyes met hers. "You need something sweet to balance out all of these practical purchases. Do you see those jars of candy over there?" She pointed to the shelf of glass jars filled with various shapes and bright colors. "Go pick out a few things for yourself." I smiled and walked toward the candy. "And if you have any brothers or sisters, get something for them, too," she said in a loud whisper.

A few times while selling our excess crops, Pa had brought us candy from his travels. Those moments were magical, each treat sweeter than the last. Now, faced with so many choices, none looked like what Pa used to bring us. I was stumped, unsure of which ones to try.

A dark-skinned boy close to my age appeared next to me, his wire-rimmed glasses perched midway down his nose. "I really like the green sugar sticks and those red candies," the boy said, pointing to each one.

I smiled. "Thanks. I couldn't decide."

The boy grinned and pushed his glasses up before walking away. I reached into the jars he'd pointed to and took out a few candies. I also took a pink lollipop I knew Kate would love—for the color, if nothing else. I carried the candies to the counter, and the woman smiled.

"These are all very good choices." She held open a small bag, and I dropped them inside. Folding the top of the bag over a few times, she said, "I believe that calls us even, if you're okay with it." She slid my purchases toward me.

"Yes, ma'am." I put the items in my pack, carefully setting the bag of candy on top. "Thank you for your help. My family really appreciates it."

She nodded and folded her hands on the counter. "We all need to do what we can to help each other. Good luck to you, son." A man approached the sales counter, so she turned her attention to him.

I practically floated out of the store. Even though I didn't have everything we needed, I had made a good start.

As I walked further into the town, I passed the remains of some burned houses and storefronts. Several of them had scorched roofs and smoke-blackened walls. Some had been so badly damaged that they stood vacant—windows broken, doors hanging open. The smell of ash and rot filled the air.

I reached a corner building where an outer wall had three long parallel jagged lines gouged into the wood. As I stopped to study the lines, I was soon joined by a freckle-faced little girl who pulled off a bite from her licorice rope.

"Whatcha lookin' at?" she asked.

I glanced at her. "These marks on the wall."

"Oh. Them's from the dragons." She noisily smacked her lips. She'd said it so matter-of-factly that I wasn't sure I'd heard her correctly.

"Dr—dragons?" My voice cracked slightly. A prickly feeling crept across my skin.

"Yep." She gave a mischievous grin, her mouth missing a few teeth. "They come every once in a while and breathe their fire on us. Don't know why. Nobody been hurt yet, but they sure do mess things up around here." When I didn't respond, she shrugged and skipped away, the licorice rope bouncing with every step.

Dragons! And not just any dragons, but destructive, fire-breathing dragons. My stomach twisted with worry as I wondered what could cause dragons to act that way. Alarm stirred in my chest. Would our next home be a place where Drake would be safe and accepted, or at least left alone?

I walked quickly down the main street of shops, stopping to offer my remaining items at those places open for business. After selling everything I'd brought and only being turned away by one grumpy shopkeeper, I now had enough coin to buy the rest of what we needed. My first purchase would be warmer clothes. As I came near the clothing mercantile, I overheard two men talking as they stood outside the store.

"Do you know what happened to that Harrings fella? I've only heard bits and pieces," one man asked, leaning against the storefront wall.

The other man shook his head sadly. "He and that character from Trulith took off together, both obsessed with finding a dragon. A couple months back, some travelers had mentioned livestock going missing a good distance away. So, they took off, planning to camp here and there until they found out what was going on. That Trulith fella got burned real bad in a fire and returned home, but Harrings hasn't been seen since."

My feet froze halfway up the steps to the store.

"You all right there, son?" one of the men called out to me.

I blinked my eyes rapidly and coughed. "Uh, yeah. Yes, sir.

Just fine." I hurried into the store trying not to think about what I'd just heard. I chose two thick blankets, and warm socks and gloves for Kate and me. A store clerk spoke with a customer while measuring fabric, and another mention of Trulith caught my attention.

"I've just returned from visiting my sister in Trulith," said the customer. The woman wore a large blue hat with a white feather that fluttered every time she moved. She held her hand to her chest and closed her eyes dramatically. "Oh, what a beautiful city it is. The roofs shine with the midday sun, sparkling like jewels."

As I paid for my purchases on the other side of the store, I heard the same customer mention a king and dragons. I couldn't hear much else, but it sounded like Trulith was a wealthy kingdom. And if they had dragons there, maybe Drake could live with them and have a normal dragon life, whatever that was. I smiled to myself as I thought about what an oddity Drake might be around other dragons, though, since he knows commands and is what Pa called "domesticated."

Before leaving town, I asked a man how far it was to Trulith. He pointed northeast, saying it was a full day's ride. I thanked him and hurried away.

The setting sun turned the sky orange and pink as I made my way back to the woods where I had left Kate. I wandered through the trees, but she was nowhere in sight. I fought a rising panic as I sped up my pace.

"Kate?" I whispered loudly, wandering deeper into the woods. My breath was tight in my throat. "Kate!"

I flinched when Buddy bounded out from behind a bush and leaped up, placing his front paws on my chest. After a few face licks, Buddy jumped down. He yipped and turned as if telling me to follow.

"Where are they, boy?"

Further into the grove of trees, I found them. Kate lay snuggled in the dragon's arms, both sound asleep. At the sight, something inside me broke. The last bit of anger I'd been holding against Drake suddenly felt so wrong. He may have caused the fires that changed our lives forever, but he loved us. There was no doubt about that.

While they slept, I repacked our belongings, keeping Kate's pack light and filling Drake's and mine as full as possible. Now, instead of our packs being filled with memories of home, they were filled with what we needed to survive.

Chapter 8

Kate was the first to see it. "Look, Zander!" she shouted, pointing at something shiny in the distance.

When we reached the top of the tree-covered mountain, I saw it, too. Ma used to describe Trulith as a kingdom so beautiful, it must have been painted with sunlight. This was it! We were almost there!

"I've never seen anything so beautiful," Kate whispered. Her smile said it all.

A strange squeak came from Drake. He seemed frozen in place. His eyes grew big as he stared at the glittering castle ahead. I grinned at his dazed reaction.

On a plateau lay the massive kingdom protected by a towering stone wall. In the heart of it, a gleaming white castle stood tall, surrounded by a mix of buildings and winding streets. The castle's corners were guarded by massive round towers, each topped with glittering metal spires flying white flags with black stars. The whole kingdom seemed to sparkle. It looked so regal, so wealthy, so impressive.

We stayed along the edge of the tree line as we walked closer. At one point, Drake, being unable to take his eyes off the kingdom ahead, ran right into the trunk of a tree. Kate giggled as the dragon vigorously shook his head.

"Feeling a bit awestruck, are you, boy?" I asked him with a laugh as I patted his neck. "It's okay. I am, too."

Knowing we couldn't just walk through the gates with a dragon, I told Kate to stay hidden in the woods so I could investigate the city.

She whined at my suggestion. "But why can't I come with you, Zander?" She twisted a strand of hair with her fingers. "I'm tired of walking and walking and only seeing grass and trees and hills. I want to see people. I want to see other children."

I squeezed her shoulders and leaned down to lock eyes with her. "I know you're ready for a change, and that's what I'm trying to make happen for us. But first, I need time to look around, and maybe find somewhere for us to stay tonight. I also need to see what the people are like. You wouldn't want to stay if everyone who lived there was mean and grumpy, would you?" I made a silly face at her. Kate laughed and shook her head. "Then you need to wait here for me. I'll be back before nightfall. I promise."

Kate nodded and gave me a hug as I stood to go, her arms gripping firmly around my waist. "Find us a good place to live, please, so we don't have to walk anymore."

She sounded so desperate—as desperate as I felt. Whatever it took, we needed this to be a place to call our home.

I pointed to the huge forest to the east of the kingdom, just like Ma had described. "Look, Kate. That forest is so big we can't even see the end of it from here. That would be the perfect place for Drake to live, wouldn't it?"

She nodded slowly, unwilling to give me the grin I was hoping for. I hugged her again before leaving her with Buddy and Drake. Wanting to get back to them as soon as possible, I moved quickly.

As I drew closer to the wall, I noticed the grass near the kingdom wall was blackened and burned. The nearby trees had been reduced to charred stumps. I wrinkled my nose at the familiar smell.

I hesitated as I approached the open gate. A guard leaned against the arched opening, picking at his fingernails and looking like he wanted to be anywhere but there. Did I need permission to enter? My mind filled with what to say if he stopped me. Taking a deep breath, I hitched my pack up higher and did my best to walk with confidence. The guard just glanced at me and nodded a single time, and I hurried on through.

As I passed through the archway, I couldn't believe the sight before me. The cobblestone road echoed with the clickety-clack of horses pulling wagons. The area bustled with people—more people than I had ever seen in one place. Adults came in and out of buildings, sometimes slowing to smile and speak to each other. Small children ran past me as they squealed and chased each other. One curly haired little boy accidentally ran into my legs while trying to keep up with the bigger kids. He stopped and looked up at me. I met his startled look with a smile, and the boy gave a little grin before running to catch up to the others.

So much movement and sound! So many buildings! Tall two-story buildings had shops below and what looked like living quarters above, some with clotheslines holding wet clothes on balconies. I saw building after building along this street. So many people. So much activity. I took a deep breath as I felt everything closing in on me. I let my breath out slowly. I couldn't panic. I had to stay focused.

Traders' carts lined one side of the main street. Their large wheels set the carts high off the ground so customers could see the goods for sale at eye-level. Several of these carts stood in front of fire-damaged buildings. Most of the carts had canvas tarps resting on poles, providing shade for the buyer and seller. Triangle-shaped pennants in various colors hung from a rope strung between the front poles, giving the area a festive feel, despite the charred rubble in the background.

Sellers called out to me as I passed. "Candles!" yelled a large man with a shiny bald head. "Made from the finest beeswax in the region!" He motioned for me to step closer to his cart full of candles, but I just raised a hand and smiled in thanks as I walked on.

"Cheese! We have the tastiest cheese in Trulith. Try a sample!" called another man. My mouth watered at the sight, but I kept going.

"Linens! The finest cloth you'll find anywhere!" The sides of this cart had long sticks holding rolls of fabric. I smiled, realizing Ma would've stopped to look through it for her next sewing project.

Walking deeper into the city, the market carts disappeared, replaced by narrow buildings of plaster and wood. The scent of fresh bread tickled my nose as I passed a bakery. Women went in and out of a general store, full baskets hanging from their arms. A black cat napped in the sunlight while lying in a store window. Men on horseback passed me, the hooves clomping on the cobblestones.

Reaching another storefront, I heard the tinkle of piano keys playing a happy tune. Laughter filled the air as I walked by. I passed a forge, where a sweaty muscular man repeatedly slammed his hammer down on metal, sparks flying.

Everywhere I looked, there was activity. Sounds and smells came from every direction. Feeling overwhelmed again, I leaned against a wall for a moment, closed my eyes, and breathed deeply.

That was when I realized this was exactly where we needed to be. Here, Kate and I could get lost in the crowd, and no one would realize we didn't have parents to take care of us. I pushed away from the wall determined to find us somewhere to live.

As I strolled, the massive castle loomed into view. It was so big! I felt small and unimportant in comparison. A stone wall only as tall as my shoulders marked the boundary between the castle and the city. Wooden bridges stretched from four evenly spaced gates in the wall, leading to the castle's fortified entrances. Beyond the wall, a deep moat circled the castle, its base bristling with wooden spikes—a clear warning to anyone thinking of causing trouble.

At the end of the main bridge, guards stood on either side of an entrance of two tall, wide wooden doors. These guards were nothing like the uninterested guard I had passed at the entrance to the city. These men stood tall and straight, swords at their sides, actively watching people as they passed by. All but the bottom edge of a metal gate hid in the stone archway above the doors, probably ready to be lowered at the first sign of danger.

The castle's towers and walls were dotted with windows—narrow slits near the base for defense, while the upper stories boasted tall glass windows that sparkled in the sunlight. As I enjoyed the impressive view, I had to shield my eyes from the glare coming from the towers' metal spires.

I didn't know how long I stood gawking at the castle before I was startled by a snort and a blast of hot air that ruffled my hair. I quickly turned and found myself practically nose-to-nose with a large black horse. The animal shifted on its hooves as I took a few steps back. The rider of the horse was a knight wearing full armor. He lifted his helmet visor, his moist brown hair sticking to his forehead.

"Sorry to have startled you, but I find myself in need of a favor." As he spoke, more riders in armor stopped behind him.

"Certainly, sir," I said, squinting to see the knight through the glare of the midday sun.

"My men and I have just returned from a long hunt and are in dire need of water. Will you bring us some from the well, so we don't have to dismount?"

"Yes, sir." I turned where the knight had pointed and saw a large well I hadn't noticed before. I tried my best not to slosh the water bucket as I carried it to him.

He waved me to the back of the group. "No, them first, please. They need it more."

I walked as quickly as I could. Some of the men had removed their helmets, cheeks reddened and sweat running down their faces. Several slouched with weariness. I set the bucket on the ground and filled the ladle before handing it to each soldier. When I reached the knight at the front of the group, I was surprised to see that, without his helmet, he looked only a few years older than I.

"Thank you," the knight said after gulping the water. "What's your name?"

"Zander."

"Zander, I am Antony, the captain of the west guard." He handed me the empty ladle.

"Nice to meet you, sir."

"You've been a great help to the soldiers of Trulith today. Maybe we'll meet again, Zander." He smiled before turning back to his men. "Forward," he called, pointing his arm toward the castle. His large black horse let out a breath as it passed me.

I stood with the bucket in my hand, watching the soldiers ride across the bridge toward the giant building. I had never seen a knight before! My parents had told me stories about their bravery, but now I had actually *met* one. I couldn't wait to tell Kate all about it.

Chapter 9

Even though I wanted to hurry back to Kate and tell her about meeting the knight, I forced myself to stay longer. I had to find a place for us to live if we were going to make Trulith our new home.

I passed the main castle bridge and followed the road which curved around part of the castle. I watched the people near me as I walked, many dressed in colorful clothes. Pretty women wearing sparkling jewels talked with each other as they strolled. Men wearing tall black hats and long fancy coats gathered in small groups for conversation here and there, sometimes breaking into laughter.

The sound of horns blowing a short tune caught my attention. Two men in black and white uniforms stood above the castle gate, the horns at their lips as they blew the melody again. The fancy-dressed women giggled excitedly, while a few of the men straightened their clothing and posture. I watched as they all crossed the bridge and entered together through the huge wooden doors which closed behind them with a heavy thud. With them gone, the area now looked rather plain and dreary.

I passed in front of a small storefront and stopped when I caught my reflection in the window. Running my fingers through my hair to try to tame it, I saw a fast movement in the glass. I turned as a pale, skinny boy with fiery red hair ran past me, clutching something to his chest. A rounder boy with darker skin and dark brown hair quickly followed behind, a big smile on his face. These two were chased by a shopkeeper, white apron over his clothes, fist punching the air.

"Stop, you boys! Thieves!" the large man yelled in a thick accent. Just after he passed me, the man bent over, hands on his knees as he tried to catch his breath. He turned and saw me. Peering through narrowed eyes, he pointed a crooked finger at me. "You! Are you with them?" he asked as he gasped for breath.

I shook my head. "No, sir. Never seen them before." I walked away slowly, trying to look like I was just out for a stroll. After passing two side streets, I glanced behind me and saw the shopkeeper crossing back the way he had come, lifting his apron to wipe the sweat from his brow. I turned left at the next street, where I'd seen the boys run.

I wondered what they had stolen. What was worth the risk of being caught? And did they have families? I wanted to find those boys. Maybe I could follow them to see where they lived. Maybe they had room for us.

I checked the small alleys and finally found them sitting on the ground with their backs against the side of a building, big grins on their faces. The red-headed boy had a bulge in the front of his jacket, his arm holding it in place.

I stood in the alley entrance. The darker boy saw me and nudged his friend. I felt the weight of their glares.

"What do you want?" the red-headed boy said with a sneer.

I shrugged. "Nothing. Just wondering what you're up to." I took a few hesitant steps toward them, waiting to see how they would react. When they didn't seem to care, I stepped closer. "I saw you running from the shopkeeper."

"Yeah? Well, he had it coming to him."

"How's that?"

The other boy spoke with an accent that was strange to me. "We're just keeping it even. He steals from people, too."

"He does? The shopkeeper?"

"Um, yeah, in a way." The red-headed boy looked down as he picked at a fingernail. "If he doesn't have enough of something that a lot of people need, he raises the price. When he does that, only the rich folks can get it, and the rest of us can't."

I saw his point. As I stood across from them, I leaned against the wall, shoving my hands in my pockets. I tried to look non-threatening.

"Who are you, anyway?" the red-headed kid asked. "I don't remember seeing you around." His eyes narrowed as he scowled. "You're not going to rat on us, are you?"

"Rat on you?" I'd never heard that phrase before.

"You know, tell the shopkeeper where we are…"

I shook my head. I walked toward them and put my hand out in greeting. "My name's Zander."

The red-headed boy stood and shook my hand, pumping it hard. "Red—you know, because of my red hair and all."

"I'm Luca," said the other boy as he shook my hand. "You not from around here?" He made an interesting sound with his r's when he spoke.

"No, I'm not," I said simply. "I'm looking for a place to stay."

"For you?" Luca asked, pointing at me. "You have no, um, no family?"

I pushed away the sadness as thoughts of my parents filled my head. "No, it's just my little sister and me."

The two boys exchanged a glance that seemed filled with an entire conversation I couldn't hear. Red nodded and said softly, "We don't have parents, either. We live with a couple of other kids not far from here, in a small abandoned building." He glanced at Luca before continuing. "We have room. If you want to try it out, we can show you where it is."

I smiled with relief. "Yes, please. That's exactly what I need."

The boys led me to a section of burned buildings in a nearly deserted area on the outskirts of the city. The building we entered sat almost hidden behind an abandoned store, as if used for storage or maybe as a shopkeeper's small home. The windowpanes were covered with curtains, hiding the view inside.

Red opened the door, using his body to force it open. "Sticks a little," he said over his shoulder.

Following Luca inside, I studied what might become our new home. Three mismatched wooden chairs and a side table stood in front of the fireplace where a small fire burned. Two closed doors along the back wall hinted of additional rooms. In the corner was a small kitchen with a table and a wood-burning stove, where a thin older girl stirred a pot.

She turned when the door opened and frowned when she saw me. Her eyes darted to the boys. I rubbed the back of my neck and looked anywhere but at her. Luca and Red took off their coats and hung them on hooks. Red took a loaf of bread out of his coat as he crossed the room and handed it to the girl, giving her a mischievous smile.

"I see you boys found a stray," she said as she pushed her curly black hair out of her face. She had dark brown skin, a shade of which I had never seen. She put the bread on the table, walked to me, and stuck out her hand. "Nyla," she said as we shook.

"Zander."

She gave me a slight smile. "Nice to meet you, Zander. You hungry? We have vegetable soup on the stove and some bread we can share with you."

"Oh, thank you, but I can't stay. My little sister's waiting on me."

"Oh." Her smile fell. "You have a family?" She shot a quick glance at Red and Luca who sat on a wooden bench at the long kitchen table.

"Um, no, just a little sister," I said quietly as my eyes studied the floor. "In fact, I need to go get her."

"She's alone?" Nyla asked.

"No, she's with our dog, Buddy. He knows how to watch out for her."

At that moment, one of the bedroom doors opened, and another dark-skinned girl came out and ran to Nyla. "A dog?" she asked with a smile. The girl was shorter than Nyla and held a well-worn doll in the crook of her arm. The girl's eyes were small and slightly slanted upward on the outer edges. Her smile lit up her round face.

Nyla gently turned the girl toward me. "Dora, this is Zander. Zander, this is my older sister Dora."

"Nice to meet you." I gave her a little wave.

Dora waved back. "You have a dog?" Her speech was different, as if her tongue were too thick to form the words.

I sensed something special about this girl. Putting my hands on my knees, I bent down to her level. "Yes, I do. He's a beautiful white dog with a curly tail."

"He sounds pretty."

"And he's very nice and smart. Do you like dogs?"

She nodded and smiled, twisting her body from side to side as she hugged her doll to her chest.

Red spoke up. "Is Buddy housebroken? We can't allow accidents in our fine accommodations, you know." Luca laughed and shoulder-bumped Red.

I smiled. "Yes, he's housebroken, and he knows commands. He won't give you any trouble. I promise."

"Then bring him. The more, the merrier, right, Nyla?" Luca asked, his eyebrows raised.

She looked at the two boys and then at me. She tried to suppress a sigh. I could tell she wasn't too sure about me. "I suppose so, but we'll just do this on a trial run. If we don't get along or if your dog causes any problems, you're out. Okay?"

I nodded. "Yes, ma'am!"

Luca and Red both guffawed. "Ma'am? She's no ma'am!" Luca exclaimed, holding his stomach as he laughed.

Nyla put her hands on her hips. "Hush up, you two. It'll be a nice change to have someone with manners around here," she said, grinning.

Chapter 10

We set up Drake's "home" in the big forest that lay to the east of the kingdom. Kate and I gathered twigs and evergreen branches and formed them into a nest for him. She pulled out the small blanket she slept with and set it inside.

"There you go, Drake," she said sweetly to the dragon, who tilted his head as she spoke. "You can have my favorite blankie to remind you that I love you."

I put a hand on Kate's shoulder. "Are you sure about leaving that? You might need it."

She looked up at me as she hugged her doll against her. "It'll be all right. I have my doll to remind me of home, but Drake doesn't have anything. I think he'll sleep better if he has it."

We set Drake's nest so deeply in the forest that it was highly unlikely Trulith citizens would find him. That meant a longer walk for us, but it was worth it to keep him safe. A clearing within the woods was nearby, which would give Drake and Buddy room to run and play when we visited. A stream gurgled alongside it, making this feel like the perfect location for our dragon.

Kate quickly grew to love the little house we lived in and the people who lived there. We did our best to blend in with the routines set by the others. After all, we were guests, lucky to have been accepted into their group. Kate enjoyed being cared for by Nyla and playing with Dora. Kate treated Dora with such gentleness, it made me proud. Even Buddy had adapted to our new home without issue.

Kate and I tried to visit Drake every day, or at least every other day. She practically demanded it, afraid Drake would forget us or need us if we didn't check on him. Buddy came along, too, and he and Drake played together with just as much enjoyment as they always had.

On our fourth day, when everyone else was out of the house, Kate sighed as she lay on the floor drawing. Buddy was sprawled out beside her. I heard the sigh but ignored it, continuing to work on the dog I was whittling out of wood. Kate sighed again.

"What?" I asked, turning to look at her. She raised her eyebrows, trying to look innocent, but she didn't fool me. "Why are you sighing?"

"I'm bored," she finally admitted, a whine in her voice.

"You're bored? But we visited Drake this morning."

"Yeah, and that's all we do. We go visit Drake, and we stay here."

A smile tugged at my lips. "I'm feeling a bit bored, too. I think we should go exploring."

Kate jumped to her feet, her face lit up with excitement. "Finally! Oh, I hope this day has a little bit of drama, but not a lot."

I had been wanting to browse in a few of the shops I'd passed the day before while asking for work. It would be good to get out. Not looking for food. Not looking for work. Not on our way to visit Drake. Just wandering for fun.

Kate and I walked to a street lined with shops. People hurried here and there. Two children chased a dog. Shopkeepers stood behind their stands or in their doorways, calling out their items for sale.

Kate took my hand and squeezed it. "I've never seen so many people!" I read the amazement on her face.

We came to a toy shop with dolls displayed in the window. Kate pulled me inside.

"Kate," I whispered, crouching down to her ear so only she would hear me, "I don't have money to spend. We can't afford any of this stuff."

"It's okay," she whispered and shrugged. "I just want to look. It doesn't cost to look, does it?" She glanced around at the other shoppers to make sure no one heard her.

I smiled. "No, it doesn't cost to look."

Kate released my hand and walked directly to a case full of dolls. She lifted one, oh so carefully, and ran her fingers over the doll's hair. She let out an appreciative sigh. "Isn't she beautiful?"

"She is," I answered, knowing that was the response she wanted.

"But I like my doll better."

That surprised me. "What? Why?"

"Because Mama made it for me. It's the only thing I have left that she made just for me." She put the doll back on the display, straightening the outfit so it looked exactly as it did before she picked it up.

I patted her shoulder, proud of her grown-up way of thinking. Before I could respond, we overheard two women talking nearby.

"Stanley says we're losing sheep. I told him he was crazy, since he'd just repaired the fence last month, but he insists that he can count, and we have two less sheep than we had a week ago."

The other woman said, "And Mable told me they're missing one of their goats."

The first woman made a "tsk" sound with her tongue. "Sounds like we have a thief."

Kate and I exchanged a knowing glance. She opened her mouth, and I slowly placed my finger on my lips, silently reminding her that we couldn't speak of Drake in front of anyone. She nodded her understanding, and we left the shop.

Passing a street vendor selling sweet rolls, the delicious smell made my stomach growl. I stuck out my arm to stop Kate.

She looked up at me with alarm. "What?"

I let a smile slowly cross my face. "I think we need a sweet roll."

Kate clapped gleefully and bounced up and down on her toes. "Oh yes! Can we?"

The vendor was a plump man with a big smile. "How may I help you, young man? Young lady?" He bowed his head slightly to each of us.

"How much is a sweet roll?" I asked as I pulled some coins from my pocket.

"You have money?" Kate asked quietly, but loud enough I was pretty sure the vendor heard.

I turned toward her and whispered, "I still have a little bit from selling our things." When the man told me the price, I moved the coins around in the palm of my hand. If I bought two, we wouldn't have much money left. Oh boy, I really needed to find some work. Trying to hide my disappointment, I said, "Um, we'll take one sweet roll, please."

The man looked at the two of us and cleared his throat. "Oh wait! I forgot. Today, I have a special—two rolls for the price of one."

Kate sucked in a breath. "Oh, thank you, thank you!" she

exclaimed as the man handed her a sweet roll wrapped in brown paper.

I paid and took my sweet roll. "Thank you, sir," I said. "Truly. That's very kind of you."

The baker blushed slightly. "Enjoy." He winked before turning to help another customer.

My heart filled as I thought about all the people who had helped us along the way—people who didn't have to, who didn't even know us, but who had good hearts and were willing to help strangers. Trulith wasn't nearly as scary as I first thought it was.

Using our fingers to pull off pieces of the sweet doughy goodness, we ate as we walked by the castle, its metal roofs gleaming in the afternoon sun. It really was an amazing sight. So grand. So perfect.

"Zander, one day, I'm going in there."

I snorted as I tried to hold back a laugh. "Inside the castle? And how will you do that? Do you see those guards?" I said pointing to the men standing at the gate. "They don't let just anybody inside the castle, you know."

She shrugged and went back to eating her roll. "I just want to see what it looks like. It must be beautiful."

We passed a colorful flowerbed along the low wall that surrounded the castle. A man was bent over, intently pulling weeds.

Kate stopped behind him. "I love your pretty flowers," she said sweetly as she ate another piece of her roll.

The man stood up but was no taller than Kate. He turned around, swiping the green cloth hat from his head when he saw us. His long strands of light purple hair swayed from the movement.

Kate giggled. "Oh, you're a little man."

I gasped and quickly put my hand over her mouth to keep her from saying more. "Um, sorry, sir."

"No apology needed, young man," he said with a grin. "I hear it often, and I take no offense." He turned to Kate and bowed slightly. "Thank you for your kind words about the blossoms. They do what they are supposed to do, and it's my job to help them along."

"Well, they really are beautiful," she said. "I'm Kate."

"Pleased to make your acquaintance," he said, bowing again. "My name is Binobrik Fizzlewhistle."

She laughed. "That's a funny name."

I rolled my eyes. "Kate!"

"It's all right," Binobrik said. "And what might your name be, lad?" he asked as he stuck his hand out to me.

I raised my sticky hand and smiled. "Sticky hand. Sorry. But I'm Zander, and it's nice to meet you, sir."

"I see you have Burt's famous cinnamon rolls. They're scrumpdiddlyumptious!" Kate giggled when she heard the word. Binobrik squinted as he looked at the sun. "I must get back to my task. It was a pleasure meeting you two. Have a good day." He waved his little fingers at us before turning back to his work.

"Bye!" Kate said with a wave. "I like that man," she whispered to me. "He's funny."

We finished eating our rolls as we walked to another market a few streets over. These buildings were cleaner and newer looking than the ones near our house. They sold better goods here, too. I would need to remember that when it was time to buy supplies.

Kate stopped to look in a store window displaying children's books when a loud horn sounded. An ear-piercing, bestial shriek came from the direction of the castle.

I ran into the street to see what was happening and gasped at the sight of a gigantic dark red dragon flying over the castle, its leathery wings flapping with ease. People screamed as they disappeared into nearby buildings. Shopkeepers immediately slammed their doors.

I turned to grab Kate, but she wasn't there.

She was gone!

"My name is Binobrik Fizzlewhistle."

Chapter 11

The shriek of the red dragon sent shivers down my spine, and I instinctively covered my ears. Another dragon came into view—big, brown, and terrifying. Its claws dangled threateningly, as if ready to capture its prey.

"Kate!" I shouted, my voice mixing with the terrified screams of humans and dragons. My entire body shook uncontrollably. "Kate!"

There was no answer.

Panic gripped my chest, making it hard to breathe. Desperation surged through me.

The brown dragon swooped dangerously low, its massive wings briefly casting a shadow over the chaos below. I felt its ferocious roar vibrate through my body.

The air filled with the heart-wrenching sounds of pain and distress as people scrambled for safety, their cries slicing through me.

I slid under an abandoned flower cart as my heart pounded. From my hiding spot, I continued searching for Kate while also keeping an eye on the terrifying attackers.

I had a clear view of the red dragon which now circled above the castle. Its broad wings pumped slowly but forcefully. The creature landed on one of the castle's pointed shiny roofs, its long claws unable to grab hold. After slowly sliding down to the edge of the roof, the dragon flapped its wings and became airborne. It flew in a circle, coming back to the same roof. The dragon leaned its head back and released an angry stream of fire. Again, it landed, tried to gain purchase on the roof, but couldn't. It let out another ear-piercing shriek. Spying a new target, the angry creature flew to a different shiny tower spire where it let out another great burst of fire, followed by a blood-chilling cry.

People screamed. I covered my ears, trying to shut out the sounds, wishing for this whole thing to be over.

I lost sight of the brown dragon until it flew toward the red one. They shrieked at each other before flying high into the sky, disappearing behind the clouds. The sky was marred by billowing black smoke while hungry flames came to life. The attack had lasted only a few minutes, but the screams of dragons and people had felt endless.

When the horn sounded again, signaling the end of the attack, doors cautiously opened, and heads peeked out to be sure it was safe. I crawled out from under the cart, my legs weak and unsteady, and the street slowly filled with people, each of us marked by the terror we had just survived.

"Kate!" I yelled, my voice cracking. "Kate!" Panic filled my chest. I had to remind myself to breathe.

The door to the bookshop opened, and Kate ran out, pushing people out of the way to get to me. She burst into tears as she wrapped her trembling arms around my waist.

"Oh, Zander! That was so scary!"

I held her tightly for a long time and then knelt to her eye-level. Wiping her tear-stained cheeks with my thumbs, I asked, "Why did you leave like that? I didn't know where you were." I tried not to sound angry but failed. My heart continued to pound like it was fighting to escape my body.

"A lady grabbed my arm and pulled me inside when the horn sounded. She held me and made me hide with her."

Realizing this had been out of her control, I nodded and tried to give her a comforting smile. I breathed slowly, trying to calm my nerves. "So you're okay?" I looked her over. "You're not hurt?"

She nodded. "I'm okay." She hugged me and nearly knocked me over, her arms wrapped tightly around my neck. "I'm sorry."

"No, no, no," I whispered. "There wasn't anything you could do. We're both safe, and that's what matters."

After a while, she loosened her grip and looked in my eyes. "They said it was dragons," Kate said softly. "But Drake would never do something like that." She paused. "Would he?"

Her sad eyes nearly broke my heart.

"No, Kate," I whispered, taking her hands in mine. "No, Drake's a good dragon." I added a smile to convince her. I hoped she wasn't thinking about our fires at home.

"Zander? I don't want to explore anymore. This day had too much drama. I want to go home now."

"Me, too. We've had enough excitement for one day."

I gripped Kate's hand tightly as we hurried back to our little house. A group of soldiers passed us, running toward the street where the brown dragon had attacked. There would be injuries needing attention, that was certain. I was so thankful for whoever had pulled Kate into the store.

We arrived to an empty house, except for Buddy whose tail wagged happily when we came in. I greeted him with a good scratching and then knelt to stoke the fire, watching the sparks as they rose from the logs.

New thoughts and worries buzzed through my head. I had it all wrong. Trulith didn't welcome dragons—they'd been *attacked* by them. The people here were terrified of dragons! How could Drake survive in a place like this? Even though he was hidden in the woods, what kind of life was that for him? Would he be happy there? Would he be safe?

My thoughts were interrupted when Kate sat in the chair next to the fireplace. Out of the corner of my eye, I saw her twirling her hair with her finger. Her chin quivered.

"Hey, what's wrong?" I crouched beside her and gently lowered her busy hand, holding both hands in mine.

"I don't want to see Drake anymore." A tear slipped down her cheek, and I wiped it away.

"Why not?"

She shrugged, looking down at the floor. Buddy lay down next to her, as if sensing her need.

"You know Drake isn't that kind of dragon, right?" I asked. She stayed silent. "He's been around humans—our own family—for most of his life. Remember the stories Pa used to tell about how Drake saved our great-great-grandpa from the bear?" Kate nodded but still didn't look at me. "Drake's a kind dragon with a big heart. Think about that. Think about how he helped our family and how he chose to live near our family even after he was healed. Think about how different, how special, that makes him from other dragons." I pressed her hands to my chest, and she looked at me. "I don't know if what we saw today is how dragons normally behave, but do you think those dragons are best friends with a *dog*?"

A smile crossed Kate's face and she let out a soft giggle. "No."

"But Drake and Buddy are best friends, aren't they?" She nodded. Buddy raised his head at the sound of his name. "I wouldn't let you near Drake if I thought he would hurt you. You know that, right?" She nodded but bit her lip. "I will always look out for you. Always. And I believe Buddy and Drake will, too."

She hugged me fiercely. "I love you, Zander," she whispered.

"I love you, too, pretty girl."

This was so hard, playing father and mother and protector to this little girl, but I adored her and would do whatever it took to keep her safe.

A short while later, the others arrived, all talking at once. They'd been in different areas of the city when the horn sounded, took cover where they could, and just happened to find each other as they returned to the house.

"Well, that was terrifying," said Red as he hung up his coat. Turning, I caught his eye and slightly shook my head. Red glanced at Kate, saw her red eyes, and gave a nod of understanding.

"Dora, honey, let's take off your coat." Nyla reached to help her, but Dora took two big steps away from her sister, crossing her arms in front of her chest. "Hey, what's wrong?"

Dora faced the wall for a moment, her head down, and slowly twisted her body from side to side. Buddy came up beside her and whined softly. She got down on her knees and patted the dog's head.

"Hi, Buddy," she said, sniffing. Putting her mouth to Buddy's ear, she whispered loudly, "Were you scared, too?" The dog licked her face repeatedly. Dora giggled and then lost her balance, falling backward as Buddy continued to lick her.

The sight made everyone laugh, including Kate. What a great sound it was.

Chapter 12

I didn't want too much time to pass before taking Kate to see Drake. Even though I knew Drake could be dangerous—he had shown that to be true in the past—she needed to be reminded that he was a friend to us, not someone to fear.

We left early the next day and were surprised to see men already cleaning evidence of the dragon attack from the castle's round towers. They certainly didn't waste any time.

Kate twirled her hair as we walked. I didn't have the heart to make her stop. I understood her nervousness.

At the open gate, we were stopped by a guard. This wasn't the same lazy guard who let us into Trulith on that first day. His upright posture and attentive eyes gave that away instantly. My senses went on high alert.

"Good morning, young people," the guard said with a smile. He kept a hand on the hilt of his sword, making it clear he knew his job. "Out to enjoy this beautiful day?"

The rigid appearance of the guard didn't quite match his overly cheerful attitude, which made me pause before answering. "We're going on an adventure in the forest."

At that moment Buddy yipped and wagged his tail at the guard.

"Well, hello there!" The guard bent down and cupped the dog's face in his hands. The man looked up at me. "This little fellow has passed through the gate a few times before. Always looks so happy when he comes back."

"That's Buddy," Kate said.

"Well, hello, Buddy," the guard said, scratching him behind the ears. He stood and waved us through. "Have a good time. Remember the gate closes at sundown. Won't be quite as easy to go in and out then."

We walked past the charred trees outside the city wall. I often checked behind us to be sure we hadn't caught anyone's attention, but the few people going in and out of Trulith stayed on the road, and we were as far from that as we could be. We hurried down the hill and across the valley to the wooded area where Drake lived. It was a long walk, which was good for Drake's safety, but it made me wish we had a horse. When we finally reached the meadow near Drake's nest, I whistled our special sound, and Drake's green snout appeared through the trees across from us. I laughed as Buddy ran across the clearing, yipping and wagging his tail, so very happy to see his friend. Drake came out of the trees on all fours, and the two played chase.

Kate bit her lip as she watched, staying close to my side. We sat on a fallen log next to the tree line. She put her cloth bag on her lap and handed me my whittling knife. She pulled out her drawing paper and pencil, dropping the empty bag to the ground. From my pocket, I pulled a short piece of wood I'd found along the way, planning to use it for a new project.

"What are you going to make?" Kate asked me as I began cutting the bark from the wood.

"I want to make something for Dora. What do you think she would like?"

"How about a bird? Birds sing, and Dora likes to sing."

"Good idea. I'll try that."

She smiled and hummed a tune while she worked on a horse she'd started drawing a few days ago.

"That's really good," I said, glancing at her picture. She just smiled and kept working.

We sat in a comfortable silence. I was glad to see Kate looking up occasionally to watch Buddy and Drake play, giggling quietly at their silliness.

As usual, my mind wandered as I whittled. I wondered if Drake had any memories of being with his own kind before he found us. Did he know his mother and father? I snickered at the thought of dragons having actual families, like a mother, father, and siblings, but then again, I didn't know any other dragons besides Drake. There were so many times I wished he could talk. I had so many questions I'd ask him.

As I watched the dog and dragon play, I realized that, yes, Drake had a family. *We* were his family, starting with my own great-great-grandfather. I wondered what would happen if Drake chose to live in the wild. We didn't hold him prisoner, and I hoped he knew that. He really was free to leave at any time.

Finally tired from playing chase, Buddy and Drake lay next to each other in the brown grass. The sun shone down on them, and the dog stretched out on his side, enjoying the sun's warmth in the chilly breeze.

A big blue butterfly caught Drake's attention as it made lazy circles in the air. He watched it intently as it landed on a wildflower. Drake rolled onto his belly and lowered his head to the ground, his eyes big and black—a clear sign he was ready to play. He lay perfectly still as the butterfly flitted nearby.

Soon, Drake lifted his head. There, on his rounded snout, was the butterfly, its wings slowly opening and closing. Drake's eyes crossed as he tried to look at it.

I nudged Kate to catch her attention. She covered her mouth and giggled at the sight.

Drake shook his head, and the butterfly took flight. The dragon rose up on all fours, and a new game of chase began. The insect flew close to him and then rose high at the last moment, as if it were teasing him. Buddy woke from his nap and watched what was going on but quickly lost interest. Drake, however, practically pranced around the meadow—if dragons could prance. Kate laughed as we watched the game, and my heart felt so full.

After chasing the butterfly for a while, Drake began snapping his mouth when the butterfly got close enough. It was then I realized that the fun game had changed. The insect mistakenly flew too close to Drake's mouth and, before I could react, he had eaten the butterfly.

Kate's mouth fell open. Drake looked around to see where the butterfly had gone. I laughed at his confusion.

She hit my arm. "That's not funny! He ate it. He killed the pretty butterfly!"

I immediately pressed my lips together but couldn't quite wipe the smile from my face. "But look at him, Kate. He didn't mean to do it." Drake walked around in a circle, looking down at the ground and then up in the air. "See? He's trying to find it."

Kate frowned and stood up with a fist on one hip, waving her finger at the dragon. "Drake. Bad boy! You don't eat butterflies!"

He stopped, tilted his head at her, and lay down on the ground right where he was. I wondered what he thought the scolding was for. Regardless, he knew she was upset.

"Hey, come here," I said to her gently. She sighed but walked over and stood in front of me. I took one of her hands in mine. "It was an accident. Just an accident." My voice cracked. Drake's past fires had been accidents, too, even though they'd had terrible results. I took a big breath and smiled at my sister. "We have to choose joy," I whispered.

She sighed softly before returning to her drawing, and her anger seemed to slowly melt away. I stopped myself from saying anything else about it. Instead, I turned my focus back to my whittling. I had nearly finished the bird when Kate put her drawing down on the log and stood to stretch.

"I'm hungry," she whined. "Can we go?"

I nodded and looked at Drake and Buddy, who had decided to investigate the clearing, their noses to the ground. I whistled to get their attention and yelled, "Come!"

Both animals raised their heads immediately and ran toward us. Buddy reached us first, his tongue hanging out and his tail wagging. Drake was on all fours as if trying to look like his dog friend.

Kate backed up behind the log as Drake drew closer.

I draped my arm over the dragon's neck and gave him a squeeze. "Bye, Drake. We'll see you next time, okay?" I knew the dragon couldn't possibly answer me, but it felt like a normal thing to say. "Kate, come tell Drake goodbye."

She backed up another step and kept her head down.

"Kate," I said softly. "Remember that you have no reason to be afraid of him." I rubbed Drake's head, and the dragon closed his eyes, enjoying the touch. "See? He's the same Drake you've always known."

She lifted her head, and a single tear trailed down her cheek as her chin quivered. Drake tilted his head and took two steps closer before gently nudging her arm with his snout. The force of the nudge moved her whole body, and she had to take a step to keep from falling over.

"Drake, stop," she said, but her voice didn't mean it.

The dragon nudged her again, and she giggled while wiping the tear from her cheek.

"See? He loves you," I encouraged.

With a smile she couldn't hide, she rubbed Drake's snout. And just like that, things had been made right again.

There, on his rounded snout, was the butterfly.

Chapter 13

Kate and I really enjoyed living with Nyla and the others, but I fought a moral battle internally each time Luca and Red stole food. They took from people who were just trying to support their families through their businesses. Nyla had a small vegetable garden behind our little house, but it didn't produce much. Pa had taught me that it was wrong to steal, so I was determined to figure out a better plan.

One day, a possible solution popped into my head, so Kate and I took Buddy to try it out.

We walked toward the butcher's shop where our experiment would take place, but my attention was drawn to the tavern across the street. A man yelled at his horse that was tied to the hitching post. The man tried to put his foot in the stirrup but missed. He muttered something and hit the horse's backside, as if blaming it for his poor aim. The large black horse neighed and took some steps to the side. The man wobbled a bit and tried again, missing the stirrup.

Kate had been watching. She grabbed my hand, saying, "He's not being nice to that pretty horse."

I bit my lip to keep from saying anything about him, knowing whatever I said would not be nice. I heard Ma's voice inside my head reminding me to set the right example for my sister. It sure was hard sometimes, though.

The man pushed his long black coat behind him, held the stirrup with one hand, and lifted his foot toward it. It took him two tries before he succeeded. Grabbing the saddle horn, he bounced on his other foot a few times before finally lifting himself up into the saddle. He took a moment to get situated, then looked around and raised his empty hands. He didn't have the reins. The horse was still tied to the hitching post.

"Forget something?" a man asked, standing on the other side of the post. He laughed, shook his head, and untied the reins. He handed them to him and ran a caring hand down the horse's mane, saying, "Starting a bit early, aren't you, Marlon?"

"Mind your own business," Marlon muttered as he abruptly yanked the reins to the side. The horse whinnied but obeyed. Marlon tugged his black hat lower over his eyes, and he and his horse sped off.

The scene brought the barn fire to my mind. Those two strangers had been wearing long black coats and black hats. What if...? *No, it couldn't be.* There were plenty of men who wore long black coats and black hats, right?

Thoughts swirled through my head until Kate tugged on my hand and said, "Come on. Buddy's ready to show you how smart he is."

As we moved toward the butcher's shop, I quickly glanced at the people walking along the street. Not one of them wore a long black coat or a black hat. I blinked hard and tried to clear my mind.

Like we had planned, I walked Buddy to the butcher's shop and had him lay under the big front window, while Kate waited in an alley across the street, slightly hidden from sight.

"Stay," I commanded while giving the dog a good scrubbing on the head. "Good boy." I smiled and ran to join Kate in her hiding place.

It was as if Buddy knew exactly what was going on. When the dog looked in the window, Kate laughed. "Look, he's making sure someone sees his sad face."

Buddy whined lightly as people walked in and out of the shop. One nicely dressed man bent to scratch Buddy behind the ears. "What's the matter, fella? You hungry?"

At that key word, "hungry," I had taught Buddy to whine and tilt his head. When he did, the man chuckled, re-entered the shop, and spoke to the butcher. The customer came out with a big raw steak and offered it to the dog. Buddy immediately took the edge in his mouth, and the man let out a big laugh.

I gave a two-note whistle, which was the signal to release the "stay." With the steak flopping in his mouth, Buddy ran across the street to our hiding place.

Kate took the meat from him while I gave Buddy a good head-scratching and a lot of praise. His curled tail swished back and forth.

We hurried home, and Nyla cooked the steak, grinning the whole time. She divided it among everyone, even Buddy. We had small portions, but no one complained.

"Ah, meat!" Luca exclaimed. He made a show of chewing noisily, rolling his eyes as he groaned with pleasure.

"And not just any ol' meat. Steak, my man! Rich people's food!" Red said. He squinted at me as he swallowed his bite. "Now tell us how you got it." After I explained Buddy's process, Red couldn't hide his astonishment. "So, your dog there is quite the actor, huh?"

    I opened my mouth to reply, but Kate beat me to it, saying, "He must have learned acting from me!"

Chapter 14

Luca burst through the door, breathing hard and looking frantic. "They got 'im!" he yelled.

We all jumped to our feet, and Dora squealed.

"Who's got who?" Nyla asked.

Luca took a few more breaths and ran his fingers through his dark brown hair as he paced the floor. "They got Red! Caught him stealing carrots. Shopkeeper's mad. I don't think he's gonna let it go this time." He threw his body into a nearby chair. "A guard came and took Red away. I got out of there as fast as I could." He bent over, holding his head in his hands.

"Why?" Nyla's voice quivered as she crouched on the floor next to his chair. "Why were you stealing? With my garden and Buddy's training, we said you wouldn't need to do that anymore."

Luca shrugged. "Red wanted to. I think he enjoys it. He likes the danger." He sighed. "And I let him talk me into it."

"Where did they take him?" I asked.

"To the castle, I guess. Isn't that where they punish people?" He rubbed his hands over his face and took a deep breath.

Dora stood behind Nyla and tapped her shoulder. "Red's in trouble?"

Nyla took Dora's hand. "Yes, he is, but we're going to help him.

Try not to worry, okay?"

Dora nodded and hugged her doll, humming quietly as she sat down at the table where Kate was drawing.

"It'll be okay," Kate said to her before turning to me. "But I don't understand. The castle's a pretty place. Why would they punish people there?"

I looked at Nyla, unsure of the answer.

"No, honey," Nyla said, "the word castle really means whatever's inside the walls. It includes everything the royal family needs, including the stables, a barn, courtyards, barracks for the guards, and, well," she glanced at me, "even the dungeons."

"What can we do?" I asked softly. "We can't just leave him there. What's the punishment in Trulith for stealing?"

Luca and Nyla gave each other a quick look before she lowered her gaze to the floor.

Luca scratched his neck, glanced at the girls, and leaned toward me. "Um, the king now has a no-tolerance view on stealing," he whispered.

I tilted my head at Luca. "And that is…?"

"Having your cheek branded."

"I don't understand."

He pointed to his cheek. "They brand you with a big X, so anyone who sees you knows you're a thief. It used to be on your hand, but people covered them with gloves or long sleeves. There's not much you can do to hide a big X on your face."

Luca's whisper might as well have been shouted from the rooftop. Warning bells clanged in my head as the words sunk in. Red would be marked for the rest of his life, for something he did as a kid.

"And you two stole over and over again? Knowing what the

punishment would be?" I asked.

Luca shrugged. "We didn't think we'd get caught. To Red, it was more of a game, and he was very good at it."

Nyla's eyes filled with tears as she wrung her hands together. "We have to help him."

"I know someone who works in the castle—a knight," I said, no longer whispering. "Maybe he can help us."

Kate turned to me. I hadn't spoken of Antony to anyone. "What? You know a knight?" she asked, her mouth hanging open.

"I met him on the first day I came to Trulith. I did something nice for him and his soldiers. He might remember me." Even as I said the words aloud, though, I doubted it. Why would a captain of the guard remember a boy he met only once?

Luca's face brightened a little. "Then we should go to the castle and find this knight friend of yours."

"I didn't say he was a friend—just that I'd met him and, you know, helped him out."

"Doesn't matter. We must try. We must do something," he said frantically as he jumped out of the chair and started pacing again.

"Sounds like we have a meeting with a knight," Nyla said with a smile as she put on her coat. "Come on, Dora. We've got somewhere to go."

"Yay!" she exclaimed, clapping her hands, always happy to get out of the little house.

The huge wooden doors to the castle entrance stood open with guards positioned on either side. One of the guards stepped in our path, a hand on the hilt of his sword.

"What business do you have within these walls?" he asked as he looked me up and down. He wore a tunic of chain mail, and his shiny helmet didn't cover the blond curls that jutted out beneath it. As he spoke, the other guard stepped toward us.

I glanced at the rest of the group and realized they were waiting for me to speak. I cleared my throat. "Please, sir, we need to speak with Antony, captain of the west guard. It's an urgent matter."

A long silence stretched before us as the guards exchanged a look. Just when I thought our request would be denied, Dora took a step forward and stood next to me.

"Hi, Thomas," she said with a sweet smile as she lowered the hood on her coat.

Immediately, the stern professional soldier turned into a regular person. "Well, hello, Dora." His smile quickly turned into a frown. "What are you doing with these people?"

"This is Nyla, my sister. Remember?" She pointed to her as Nyla gave a small wave.

The guard grinned and bowed his head slightly. "Miss Nyla, forgive me. I didn't see you."

A slight smile tugged at her lips. "Thomas," she said with a nod.

Thomas turned to the other guard. "It's all right. Let them pass."

"Where will we find Antony?" I asked him.

"Go through the next gatehouse and across the courtyard. When you enter the building, turn left at the second corridor," he said as he pointed, "and wait in the first room on the left. There are a table and chairs where you can wait. We'll let him know you're here."

The other guard called out to a boy standing nearby who looked younger than I. After receiving his whispered instructions, the boy nodded and ran in the direction we were headed, disappearing around a corner.

As we walked, Luca wiggled his eyebrows at Nyla and grinned.

"You have something to tell us?"

She laughed and pushed him, making him almost lose his balance. "You know that Miss Glenda, the healer, has been training me when she has time. I went with her to help Thomas's family after a dragon attack. It was nothing."

"Thomas doesn't seem to think it was nothing," Luca teased.

A group of horses passed by, hooves clacking on the stone-paved path. Their riders wore knights' cloth tunics of black and white, the colors of Trulith. I looked for Antony, but he wasn't among them.

When we entered the building, I smiled as Kate's eyes took it all in.

She yanked excitedly on my arm. "Zander, I finally get to see inside the castle, just like I said!" Her face lit up with her smile.

It was a grand building. Its white walls held banners and embroidered tapestries of black and white. Sounds echoed off the stone floor and high ceilings. Everyone walked with purpose. Some women wore silks and jewels, while others wore regular work dresses like Ma used to wear.

I glanced at my friends behind me and noticed they didn't seem nearly as in awe of the sights as I was.

"Have you been in the castle before?" I asked them.

"You forget that we've lived here for several years," Nyla said. "In fact, part of the king's birthday festival is held inside the castle walls. It's the one time each year when the gates are open to everyone in Trulith."

We reached the room where the guard had told us to wait. Just as we sat down around the large table, a young boy stepped into the doorway.

"Are you the ones seeking Sir Antony?" he asked in a high voice.

"Yes," Luca said.

"He'll come as soon as he can." The boy bowed slightly and then left.

The time passed slowly as we waited. We'd grown tired, but just as Luca suggested we leave, Antony appeared in the doorway, wearing the black and white tunic we'd seen other knights wearing. We stood when we saw him. He glanced at each of us and smiled when he saw me. It took only a few long strides for him to cross the room to me.

"Young man, it's good to see you again," Antony said as we shook hands.

"Yes, sir. I'm Zander, if you recall." I introduced each of the others. "We have something important to discuss with you."

"How may I be of assistance?" Sir Antony asked, concerned, as he took the remaining empty chair. "Please, everyone, sit." He smiled at each of us, giving a wink to Dora, who giggled and ducked her head.

I explained the situation, pointing out that Red was only twelve years old and was just trying to feed us. Nyla sniffed and wiped a tear. When I finished, Antony sat quietly, scratching the stubble on his chin.

"I'm not sure what I can do to help your friend," he said. "But due to his age, perhaps the king would see him as a child getting into mischief instead of a man doing harm. But I must ask you: if Red is released, what will keep him from stealing again?"

Luca spoke up. "Sir, we may not be the most honorable in Trulith," he said humbly, looking at his folded hands on the table. "Sometimes we struggle to get what we need. But if Red can be released unharmed, I promise we'll find a way to be better, to stop stealing." He looked up at the knight in a sincere appeal.

"Please, sir. He's my best friend. He has no one looking out for him but us."

Antony looked at me. "Is that true? He's alone?" I hesitated and then nodded. The knight looked at each of us individually. "Are you alone? All of you?"

Kate sat up straighter in her chair and spoke up. "I'm not alone." She leaned her body closer to mine. "Zander's my brother. We're a family."

"Actually, we're all a family," Nyla said to the knight, "all six of us." She blinked away tears. "We're not a typical family, but it works for us. I've grown to love each of them as I would my own family."

Luca reached his hand over to hers and gave it a squeeze. Dora, sitting on Nyla's other side, did the same.

Antony tapped his fingers on the table. "It sounds like you look after one another." We nodded. He took a deep breath as he leaned back in his chair, one arm resting on the table. "Zander, do you steal like Red does? To survive?"

I swallowed and cleared my throat. "No, sir. I've not had to yet."

I knew how often I'd thought about it since Pa died, though. Who knows what I might have had to do if our house hadn't caught fire, forcing us to leave? We might have starved if we'd stayed.

"Then we must do our best to keep it that way." Antony slapped his palm on the table as if he had come to a decision. "I'll approach the king on your behalf and plead the boy's case, requesting no punishment, as long as Red agrees to a condition." He looked at Luca and me. "My west guard is in need of dependable assistance with the horses and such. If you boys and Red agree to work for me, I'll do this for him."

Luca's eyebrows furrowed. "But why should all three of us work for Red's punishment?"

Antony leaned forward in his chair. "I'm trying to help you. I can see you're struggling. I assume you want to stay out of the orphanage. Correct?"

"Yes, sir," Luca said emphatically.

"You'll work for me five mornings each week—with pay, of course."

"You will pay us?" Luca asked.

Antony laughed. "Yes, I'll pay you. That way, you can continue to live with your family and won't need to steal from the citizens of Trulith. What do you say?"

Luca stood up from his chair so quickly, it screeched across the wooden floor. He reached out his hand to the knight. "I say yes! And thank you!"

I agreed, too, and assured Antony that Red would agree as well.

After exchanging grateful handshakes and getting a heartfelt hug from Dora, the knight left to deal with Red's situation.

As we walked home, I held Kate's hand, swinging my arm high, forward and backward, which made her laugh.

"I'm so happy that worked out," Kate said with a smile. "And now you have a job. It was a good thing you met that knight when you did."

"Yes, pretty girl. A very good thing."

Chapter 15

The day after Red was released from jail, the boys and I rose early and reported to the castle gates. My stomach swirled with nerves, even though I was eager to work and be able to buy what we needed.

A bitter chill had settled on Trulith. I tightened the belt around my coat and shoved my hands into my pockets. The threat of snow lingered in the air like a heavy blanket.

After telling the guard at the entrance gate the reason for our visit, a young boy escorted us to a room to wait. Antony arrived promptly, smiling as he shook our hands. He told us we'd be working in the stables. The horses all needed to be brushed, the hay removed and replenished, and there would be other chores as well. Antony said several stablemen had left the castle to work for the newly married Baron Whitefield. Forming a new household often left the castle short-handed at times, but Antony explained that everyone was free to choose for whom they worked; it wasn't unusual to have hired hands leave to work elsewhere. After introducing us to the stable master, he left.

It was a long morning full of hard labor, but I enjoyed it. I'd been feeling sort of useless the past few weeks, not having much to show at the end of the day but a few whittled animal shapes. It felt good to do something helpful. By morning's end, we were all exhausted and sore from the physical labor, but when I headed home, I walked with my head held high and a satisfied grin on my face.

I liked my mornings working in the stable—except for the smell of manure. Even though I'd been around farm animals my whole life and loved taking care of them, I doubted I'd ever get used to the stench.

Kate and I made a point to visit Drake in his forest at least every couple of days. Our visits with him always lifted our spirits. She wanted to go every day, but I was afraid of attracting someone's attention, and that was the last thing we needed. We made sure to stay unnoticed, often changing our routes and the times we traveled.

One afternoon, Kate and I left the city to visit Drake, with Buddy happily trotting ahead of us. When we finally reached the meadow in the woods, we called out, but Drake didn't show himself. My mind filled with worry as we looked for him. Buddy led the search and barked for us to follow him further into the woods.

I stopped when we reached a large, burned section of another clearing deeper in the forest. The air smelled of ashes. My stomach churned at the thought of what we might find. What would have been brown grass was now black. Bushes and low-lying trees had become leafless twigs.

Kate's footsteps slowed. A silent "wow" formed on her lips.

Looking closer, I saw dirt scattered along the outer edge of the blackened field. Drake must have used the dirt to put out the fire. I grinned. Smart dragon.

I turned at the sound of rustling leaves. Drake poked his head through some bushes, his body hidden. It looked like a floating dragon head in a sea of leaves.

"I see you were busy while we were gone," I said.

"Did you do this?" Kate asked him, hands on her hips in a stern motherly fashion.

Drake glanced at the damaged area. He lowered his head and blinked slowly. I walked to the "floating head" and gave it a good rub. Drake leaned into my hand and then came out of the bushes.

"I think it was an accident." I tapped Kate's shoulder and pointed. "See where he tried to put it out with the dirt? And look at him. You can tell he's sorry for it."

"Oh," she said softly before giving Drake a hug. "I bet that was scary, huh?" She let go and turned back to me. "Remember a long time ago when he set Papa's potato field on fire from a sneeze? And then you and Papa ran around like crazy trying to put out the fire?" She laughed so hard, it made me laugh, too.

"Yeah. I also remember he wasn't happy about losing part of his crops."

"But the potatoes came in better the next year." She shrugged. "Everything worked out. Papa said so."

Our conversation was interrupted by the faint sound of the Trulith horn.

Kate grabbed my arm. "Another attack?"

We ran through the woods, followed closely by Buddy and Drake. Just before we reached the forest's boundary, I extended my arms to block the others from going beyond the last line of tall bushes. A mournful groan came from Drake as we stood in silence, watching the scene unfold before us.

This time, Trulith's enemies were different dragons. The biggest dragon flapped its dark green wings as it flew close to the castle's pointed turrets. The sun's reflection shone brightly on the metal roofs. The dragon landed awkwardly on one, craning its long neck to get a closer look at the sparkling surface. It shrieked its annoyance, loud enough that we heard it all the way to the forest. A large brown dragon landed on a roof near the first one and did the same.

My breath caught as my mind buzzed with a new idea. "Oh, I understand! They think it's treasure."

"Treasure?"

"Most dragons are attracted to shiny things, like jewels and gold…you know, treasure. At least, that's how it is in the stories Pa told me. Maybe they think the shiny roofs are a treasure they want to take with them."

The green dragon let out another screech. Then the dragons took flight, joined by a small brown dragon and a much smaller green one.

"Oh, look. Baby dragons!" Kate said gleefully. But her joy turned to fear when the dragons circled back and swooped down toward Trulith. The two larger ones blew streams of glowing flames as they flew, leaving trails of burning roofs behind them. The two smaller ones screeched, trying to keep up with the others.

Drake never took his eyes off the dragons but let out another quiet groan.

Hearing the people's distant screams made my mind jump to Nyla, Dora, Red, and Luca. I hoped they'd found shelter and were safe from the dragons' attack.

"All those people." Kate's voice quivered. She squeezed my arm. "The dragons are hurting them."

We both jumped when Drake let out a loud roar. Never before had I heard such an intense sound come from him. He stood on his hind legs, back straight, neck extended. His head tilted up to the sky as he released another fierce cry. I looked back to the city and saw the dragons' heads turn in our direction. Drake was calling to them!

"Get down!" I pushed Kate to the ground. "Down!" I directed the dog and dragon. Both followed the command immediately. Drake looked at me, his eyes mournful. "Stay," I whispered.

What would we do if the dragons flew to our forest? Drake would be found, and everything would be ruined. I held my breath as I pushed twigs aside to peer through the bushes. In the distance, I saw the faint outline of four tiny figures in the sky, wings flapping as they flew away in the opposite direction. Streams of black smoke billowed above the city walls.

I jumped into action. "We have to go," I said to Kate. "They close the city gates soon after an attack to keep looters from coming in. We have to get there before they're closed."

We quickly told Drake goodbye, and I gave him the "home" command and pointed to his section of the forest, thankful I'd spent some time teaching him that word on an earlier visit. Drake didn't understand why we were leaving, but I couldn't explain further. I smiled and patted his neck, hoping that was enough.

Kate and I ran to the city, Buddy bounding happily around us, unaware of what was going on. Once inside the city gates, chaos erupted as soldiers and shopkeepers worked side by side to put out fires. A line of people holding full buckets formed behind them. Children cried. Injured people sat in the streets as healers did their best to help them.

We hurried home, and when I saw our little house unharmed, my knees wobbled in relief. Thankfully, our friends had been at home when the horn sounded. After sharing hugs of relief, we gathered at the kitchen table and drank mugs of warm tea. I hadn't even realized how cold I'd been during all of this. The warm liquid soothed me as it went down my throat.

"Did you see the dragons?" Nyla asked. I nodded as I took another sip from my mug. "Were you hurt? Are you okay?"

"We're fine," I said. "We were out in the woods. We hadn't been there for very long when we heard the horn. We saw the whole thing." I cupped my hands around the warm mug and shook my head. "A terrible sight..."

Without hesitation, Kate burst out, "There were two big ones and two little ones. Dragons, I mean."

"Two little ones?" Luca looked up, frowning. "There are more?" He clenched his fists.

Red spoke up. "Calm down, Luca. The soldiers will catch them."

Luca's face reddened. "Really? You think so? They haven't found them yet, have they? And how many more attacks will there be before then, huh?" He stood abruptly, making his chair tip over. Luca growled as he grabbed his coat and went outside, slamming the door behind him.

The soldiers were searching for *dragons*? That's what they'd been hunting all along?

A small moan escaped Dora. Nyla rubbed her sister's back to calm her. I looked expectantly at Nyla, waiting for an explanation.

"Luca lost a good friend during a dragon attack," she explained. "The kid was in a shop when it caught on fire. Couldn't get out." She shook her head sadly. "Luca's still not over it."

Remembering Pa's death in the fiery barn, my heart hurt for Luca and what he'd been through.

Sensing my sadness, Kate climbed into my lap and leaned her head against my chest. I curled my arms around her and gave her a hug as she twirled a section of her hair.

Softly, I told Nyla, "Our pa died in a fire a few weeks before we had to leave our home." I gently lowered Kate's hand and patted her arm to calm her.

Dora put a hand on Kate's back. "I'm sorry," she said softly.

Red lowered his fist to the table with a thud. His cheeks were flushed. "Filthy dragons." He stood and paced the floor. "This is the fourth time they've been here in less than a year. They destroy and kill, and then they leave. What do they want? Why do they come here?" He threw his hands up in outrage.

I was about to explain my thought about the castle roofs attracting them when Kate pulled away from my hug. "Not all dragons are bad," she told Red with a frown.

I pulled her against my chest again and shushed her gently. I felt the stares of the others but didn't raise my eyes to meet them. An explanation would be required if I did.

Running a hand through his hair, Red sighed and said, "I'm sorry, Kate. Maybe you're right. There might be some good ones out there, but they're not the ones attacking us." He put on his coat. "It's getting dark. I'm going to find Luca."

"Do you want me to come with you?" Nyla asked as she took the mugs to the wash basin.

He shrugged. "Sure. Then we can split up and cover more ground."

Dora eagerly went with them. Once they left, the silence of the house closed in on me. The wind had picked up, making a howling noise as it passed through cracks. I added wood to build up the fire while Buddy stretched out in front of it, instantly falling asleep after the day's excitement.

I washed the cups and tried to quiet my mind while Kate sat on the floor, watching the fire as she pet Buddy.

After a while, Kate yawned and stretched. "I'm tired."

I picked her up, and we sat together in front of the fire. "It was a busy day, wasn't it?"

She nodded as she curled up against me. "Do you think Papa would have known how to make the dragons go away?"

I thought about it for a moment. "I don't know. He knew a lot about Drake and how to care for him, but I'm not sure he had any experience with dragons like these."

"I miss Papa," she said sleepily, ending it with another yawn.

"Me, too, Kate. Me, too."

It looked like a floating dragon head in a sea of leaves.

Chapter 16

The next few days were busy with clean-up efforts throughout the city. Nyla took the girls to the castle to help with the injured, assuring me that Kate would be with her the whole day and wouldn't leave her sight. Kate was excited about getting to help people, but she quietly admitted that she was afraid the mean dragons would come back. Honestly, that thought was never far from my mind, either.

We boys reported to the stable as if it were any regular workday but soon realized that nothing was "regular" after a dragon attack. We worked in the stable for about an hour before Antony came in. He wore a heavy tunic over his clothing, the knight insignia on the left chest. Even though his sword hung at his side, he looked like he was ready for a workday, whatever that might include.

"You are just who I was looking for," Antony exclaimed when he saw us. "Put your tools away and come with me," he insisted with a repeated wave of his hand. "There's a lot of work to do, and we need everyone's help. Are you up for it?"

Luca threw down his shovel. "I'll gladly do anything that doesn't involve horse droppings!"

We removed our work aprons and eagerly followed Antony as

he led us out of the castle.

"Sir...," Red said. Antony stopped and faced us. "Did you hear that noise at the end of the attack? The noise that seemed to scare the dragons away?" Red looked at Luca and me, as if seeking confirmation. I kept my face blank. "It almost sounded like another dragon in the distance. When they heard it, they flew away."

My heart beat so loudly, I thought for sure they'd hear it.

Antony nodded. "Yes, there's been a lot of discussion about what that might have been. Any ideas?"

I stuck my hands in my pockets and shrugged. *I* certainly wasn't going to say anything. Red and Luca didn't seem to have any ideas, either.

"Well, regardless, I'm glad to see you boys are unharmed," he said over his shoulder as he began walking again. "We've not had attacks so close together before. We just can't seem to figure this out. They always arrive from the west, which is where we've been searching, but we've been unable to find their nests. And we don't understand what's bringing them here. Why do they come?"

"Antony," I said meekly, "how long have you had the metal roofs on the castle?"

"About a year. The king had them installed in recognition of his coronation anniversary last year. He likes things that sparkle and shine. He's quite proud of the way the metal roofs gleam when the sunlight hits them. Why do you ask?"

I rubbed the back of my neck as I paused to gather my thoughts. "Stories say that some dragons are attracted to shiny things, like jewels and gold. Maybe when the sun hits the metal roofs, it grabs their attention and lures them to Trulith."

Antony looked at me for a moment. "I hadn't considered that."

He clapped his hand on my back as if we were old friends. "Well done."

"Maybe you could cover the roofs with mud," Red said with a laugh. "We have plenty of that around here."

Antony grinned, his eyes sparkling. "Psh. As if the king would consider putting mud on his pristine castle." He grew serious and rubbed his chin. "It is something to consider, though."

When Antony slowed his pace, I realized we'd reached our destination—a storefront that had caught fire during the dragon attack. My nose wrinkled at the bitter smell of ash and smoke. The entire front of the store had been burned, a scorched mess of wood and ashes left in its place. Burned and broken timbers from the roof had fallen inside, and the sun shone down through the holes. Charred shoes littered the floor. This shop owner lost his entire source of livelihood from this short but brutal dragon attack. I hoped the owner was unharmed.

"Here we are, gentlemen," Antony said, rubbing his hands together. "I've seen how well you three work together, which is why I'm asking you to focus your efforts here."

"What exactly are we to do?" Red asked. "This place is pretty much destroyed."

"I need you to go through everything inside. Sort items into what is destroyed, what's fixable, and what's usable as it is. Usable ones will, no doubt, smell like smoke, but hopefully it's nothing some fresh air won't fix. This shoemaker will have no income while he recovers from his injuries, so if we can salvage any of his goods to sell in a temporary location, that could mean the difference between his family going hungry and not."

"We'll do it, sir," I said.

Antony smiled and clapped me on the back again. He seemed

to do that a lot. "Excellent!" he said with a smile. "I'll have our food wagon come by to provide you with a mid-day meal while you work."

"You're feeding us?" Luca asked.

"The royal family believes it's their duty to bring the kingdom back to full working order as soon as possible, and that includes taking care of those willing to help in the restoration effort." He paused and looked at each of us. "You are very good workers. I've heard it from the stable master, and I've witnessed it myself. Let me know once you've sorted the goods, and I'll send a cart to gather the usable items. I suspect you'll be finished shortly after midday. When you're done, you may go home. I'll find you in the stable tomorrow morning to give you your next assignment."

Two mornings later, we had almost finished our shift in the stables when several soldiers rode in. After dismounting, they removed their helmets and waited for the rest of their group to come in. Each man looked tired and frustrated.

Luca and Red quickly led the horses to their stalls and removed their saddles, while I made sure each had fresh hay and water.

"Where else is there to look?" asked one man, his curly black hair shimmering with sweat. "I feel like we've searched everywhere—every mountain, every cave, every hole big enough. There's no nesting area to be found."

I saw Red and Luca exchange looks. They were listening, too.

Another soldier sat on a stool and leaned against a wall. "All I want to do is find those dragons and kill them, every last one of them. For my Maggie, if for no other reason."

"And for my father's business that burned to the ground after the first attack," said another. "He still hasn't recovered from it financially. I don't know if he ever will."

At that moment, Antony walked into the stable, his helmet tucked under one arm while holding his horse's reins in the other hand. His men immediately stood. He waved a hand of recognition, and they relaxed and returned to what they'd been doing. I led Antony's horse to a stall.

"Listen, men," Antony began, "I know you're all tired. Our search seems unfruitful and endless." He walked slowly among his men. Luca, Red, and I tried to look busy as we listened. "There must be a dragon lair somewhere, though, and I intend to find it. We've tried traps. We've tried arrows. Nothing seems to work. So, we must find where they're living. This is for our families. We will continue our search until we have found and defeated the enemy. Agreed?"

"Yes, sir!" the men yelled in unison.

"You're all free to go. We started extra early today, so get some rest. We'll meet back here tomorrow at sunrise."

The men talked softly among themselves as they left the stable. Antony patted their shoulders with appreciation as they passed by.

After the last man left, Antony turned to us. "Thank you for taking such good care of the horses so they're ready and rested when we need them. You're doing an important work for us," he said as he left.

I stood a bit taller, feeling proud of my efforts.

"Did you hear that?" Red asked. "They don't even know how to kill the dragons. Traps and weapons have failed. How will they get rid of them even if they find them?"

    A whirlwind of worries circled through my mind—dragon hunting, dragon attacks, Drake's safety, and a dozen other things. I wish I knew what to do.

Chapter 17

"So have you heard the news?" Luca asked just before shoving a large piece of bread into his mouth.

I doubted I'd ever get used to watching Luca eat. He took huge bites of everything. And even worse, he pushed the food into his cheeks and talked when his mouth was still full. It sure made him hard to understand. At least food didn't fall out when he was talking.

"The dragon reward is bigger." Luca smiled and elbowed Red. "We should go on a dragon hunt. We could catch those filthy creatures and get rich at the same time."

Kate looked at me, her mouth hanging open. I purposely ignored her. My mind filled with its own set of gasp-worthy thoughts, like I hadn't realized there was a reward being offered for dragons. That put everything in a new light—a terrifying new light, as far as Drake's safety was concerned.

Nyla chimed in. "Really? So that's what all the hubbub was about outside the castle today."

"Hubbub?" Luca raised an eyebrow and shrugged. "I don't know that word, but the king has doubled the reward. Doubled!" He took a bite of his meat and chewed for a moment. Waving his fork in the air for emphasis, he said, "I don't know how to kill a dragon, but a double reward makes me want to try."

Red sat back and folded his arms. "Nobody even knows where they're coming from, except 'from the west,' like Antony said. Besides, the king's knights should be the ones hunting the dragons, not every untrained person in the kingdom."

Nyla added, "I agree. If every man grabs a weapon and goes on a hunt, someone's going to get hurt…or worse. I'd rather not have to stitch men up after their bodies are sliced open by a dragon's talons."

Red leaned forward with his elbows on the table. "Zander, you're being quiet over there. What do you think?"

My cheeks heated under everyone's intense gaze. I cleared my throat. "I think Nyla's right. I think the dragons that attacked Trulith are dangerous and need to be caught by trained soldiers, not by a baker or a shopkeeper or a bunch of kids. People could get hurt or even killed, and we don't need any more of that."

Nyla and Kate both nodded their agreement. Dora watched Kate and then nodded, too.

Luca took his empty plate to the wash basin. "You do what you want, but *I* feel like doing some dragon hunting." He scratched his belly as he headed to the door. "Thanks, Nyla, for dinner. Delicious, as always." He shrugged his coat on.

"Where are you going?" Nyla asked over her shoulder as she walked to the kitchen. "It's a little late to be going out, isn't it?"

He smiled at us as he opened the door. "If I'm going to catch a dragon, I must learn how it's done. I will go to the tavern. Some gentlemen there might know how."

After he closed the door, Nyla scoffed. "Well, he certainly won't find any 'gentlemen' at the tavern." Red snickered as he joined her to wash the dishes. "And I doubt anyone there knows about catching a dragon, either."

I took my dishes to them and then sat in front of the fire to whittle. Considering the dragon-heavy topic at dinner, I wasn't surprised when Kate joined me. I put down my whittling, and she climbed on my lap. Putting her arms around my neck, she whispered in my ear, "They won't catch Drake, will they?" She leaned back to see my face, and I noticed tears forming in her eyes.

"I don't think so," I whispered back. "Drake knows how to hide. And he's fast, even though he flies low. Something everyone seems to have forgotten is that you can't really sneak up on a dragon to catch one. He'd probably hear you before he saw you."

Kate blinked her tears away and twisted her mouth in thought before giving me a shaky smile. "You're right."

"I'm worried about Drake being seen, though." I shrugged. "Maybe we should leave Trulith and look for a safer place for him to live—a safer place for all of us to live."

"Nooo," she whined out loud. As soon as she realized what she'd done, she looked at Red and Nyla to see if they'd heard her. Luckily, they were talking as they washed the dishes. "Sorry," she mouthed to me. She leaned in again and whispered, "I like it here. I don't want to leave."

I pulled her in close for a long hug. Staring into the fire, I worried about the only two options we seemed to have: stay and risk Drake's safety, or leave and risk not finding as good a home for Kate as what we have here.

"I'm going out to find Luca before he gets into trouble," Red called out as he pulled on his coat and slipped out the door.

"What are you two whispering about in here?" Nyla teased as she came to sit near the fire, holding her latest embroidery project.

Kate released her hold on me and kissed me on the cheek before getting down from my lap. "Just some brother-sister talk." Kate left the room with Dora right behind her.

Luca and Red came back an hour later. Kate and Dora were already asleep.

"So, did you find what you were looking for?" I asked over my shoulder, my eyes trained on my whittling project.

"Huh?" Luca asked.

"How to catch a dragon…"

"Oh, um, not really."

Red snickered. "I doubt any of those men have ever left the city walls, let alone gone dragon hunting."

Luca stood in front of the fire, his palms open to the heat. "They all had different ideas of the best way to do it, but they were just ideas."

"And what did they say?" I had never given it any thought before, but learning how men hunt dragons might help me keep Drake safe.

"One man said you set 'em afire." Red said. I couldn't hold back a laugh. "What's so funny?"

"If dragons could catch on fire, they'd be lighting each other up with their breaths. Their hides are much too tough for that. I'm sure their scales are fireproof."

Luca studied me for a moment before continuing. "Okay…and another man said to shoot it with iron arrows."

"Again, I'm sure their hides are too thick."

Red narrowed his eyes. "Do you have some first-hand knowledge of dragons we don't know about?"

Uh oh. I'd gone too far. "What?" I tried to look innocent. "I don't know what you're talking about. How would I know how to kill a dragon? Psshhh." Realizing it was better to end the conversation, I faked a yawn and put my whittling project aside. "I'm going to bed. See you in the morning."

I tried to walk normally but felt like I couldn't get out of the room fast enough. I was glad Kate wasn't nearby for that discussion, or she might have revealed even more than *I* did. I would have to remind her that we must not talk about dragons when anyone is nearby. For Drake's safety. And for ours.

Chapter 18

Although the stable was full of contented horses, there was one cantankerous black horse named Midnight that never seemed to relax. He appeared skittish, alert to the slightest sound, and had to be kept apart from the other horses because he made the rest of them nervous. Nial, another stable hand, had warned us to keep our distance from the horse, saying someone had been injured after getting too close. We were told to clean Midnight's stall the best we could and make sure he had fresh hay and water, but otherwise leave the horse alone.

"He doesn't get turned out with the others?" Red had asked.

Nial shook his head. "No. His owner doesn't want him to have any interaction with the other horses. Downright mean man, he is."

I felt sorry for Midnight and wondered who he belonged to. Even after all this time working in the stable, I hadn't seen anyone ride him. No wonder the horse was unhappy.

After several days of watching Midnight from a distance, I couldn't stand it any longer. I approached the horse slowly while encouraging him with a soft voice. He watched me and whinnied, raising his head up and down. I held an apple in my open palm, and he took a long look at the offering. I continued to talk softly and extended my hand as I came closer. Finally, Midnight smelled the apple and took it, munching lazily while I lightly patted his neck.

"That's a good boy," I praised, rubbing the horse gently with both hands. Footsteps sounded behind me.

"Look at you," Nial said. He stood with his hands on his hips. "I don't know how you got close enough to actually touch him. I tried for weeks with no progress. Finally just gave up. Ornery one, that one." He gave a crooked smile and returned to his chore.

"I think maybe you're just misunderstood," I whispered to Midnight as I stroked his neck. The horse bobbed his head, his wavy black mane rippling with the movement.

The next day, I won over Midnight with yet another apple and a gentle rubbing. When I placed a brush against the horse's side, the muscles beneath his black hair shuddered.

"Shhhh," I whispered, rubbing the horse with one hand as I lightly brushed him. After a few brush strokes, Midnight let out a sigh. I whispered to him as I worked, pleased that I could bring some peace to the animal. I had almost finished brushing him when I heard boots skid to a stop behind me.

"What do you think you're doing?" someone scolded.

Midnight's attitude changed upon hearing the man's voice. What had been a calm horse only moments before was now an agitated animal with wide eyes. His hooves shuffled as he shifted position.

My heart raced as I turned. In front of me stood a man wearing a long black coat and a wide-brimmed black hat. Oily black hair covered one side of his face, making only one eye visible. That one eye had dark, tired circles beneath it but, at the same time, held a crazed, angry look.

This was the man from the tavern.

This might be the man who attacked Pa to get to Drake!

I quickly put the brush on a shelf as I tried to hide my unease. "I was just brushing him. Is he yours?"

The man opened the stall gate and threw a blanket on the back of the horse. "Yes," he muttered gruffly. "And don't mess with him. He doesn't need brushing. He doesn't need your attention. Just leave him alone, and I'll deal with him." He paused briefly, peering at me through his squinted eye. "Do I know you?"

"Um, I don't think so. I'm Zander. I work here." I glanced at Luca and Red, who had stopped working to watch.

"You look familiar." He made a grumbling noise before heaving the saddle onto Midnight's back and roughly latching the buckles. Grabbing the horse's reins, he nearly ran into me as he turned to go. "Move or I'll run you over," he grunted as he pulled the horse from the stall.

Midnight raised his head in the opposite direction, fear in his eyes.

My heart hurt for the horse. "He's a good horse. He should be treated kindly."

As soon as the words left my mouth, the man swung around, his face only inches from mine. "This is *my* horse. *My* property. And you will leave him alone, *or else*..."

Luca and Red now stood beside me.

"Or else, what?" Luca asked, gripping a pitchfork.

With my friends next to me, I stood taller. The man glared at each of us and turned to leave the stable, yanking the horse to follow. Midnight whinnied loudly and lifted his head in defiance.

"You don't have to act like that to get a horse to do what you want." Red's eyes blazed in an unspoken challenge.

The man didn't respond but shot Red a warning look as he mounted his horse at the stable doors. We stood beside the empty stall and watched in shock as Midnight reared up on his hind legs, throwing his rider to the ground. The man landed on his side with a thud and took a moment before getting up.

Three older men passed by, and their laughter echoed through the hall. "What's the matter, Marlon? Can't control your own horse?" one muttered.

Between snickers, another man said, "I bet he's heading off to slay a dragon. Am I right?" The man looked at Marlon as if expecting an answer.

"Mind your own business, old man," he muttered as the men walked on. As soon as he stood, his hand went to his face, making sure his hair covered his eye. He roughly brushed himself off, pausing only long enough to send a glare my way. He grabbed Midnight's reins and limped as he led the horse away.

"That man...," Luca muttered as he returned to his work.

I tugged on Red's arm. "Hey, what did he mean about going to slay a dragon?"

Red shrugged. "I don't know. Maybe he's hunting dragons for the reward."

Nial grabbed a pitchfork and entered Midnight's stall. "Yeah, Marlon's made it his mission to kill every dragon in the land. The king has offered a big reward for each dead dragon, and Marlon seems determined to collect."

I leaned against a railing, my heart thumping loudly. My palms felt sweaty and cold. "Do you think he will? Kill a dragon, I mean."

"He'd have to find one first. He did get burned while hunting a dragon a few months back. Claims a dragon did it, but he probably just fell into his campfire and didn't have the guts to tell anyone the truth." Nial snorted as he mucked out the stall. "Everyone says Marlon's crazy."

My thoughts were a jumbled mess, crashing into each other like waves in a stormy sea. My stomach felt twisted like a knot.

Could it be? Was Marlon at our barn that night? Had he somehow known Drake was inside?

I needed an answer to the most important question swirling inside me, and the only way to get it was to be brave and ask, even if the answer could change everything for Kate and me. I forced my mouth into a flat, expressionless line, not wanting any of my inner turmoil to show on my face.

"Do you feel safe living in Trulith?" I asked my friends. "I mean, with the dragon attacks and all, do you feel safe?"

Luca patted my shoulder. "This whole land has dragon troubles. I've heard you must travel over the rock-covered mountains in the north to reach a place that hasn't seen dragons."

"And that's over a month of travel—even more if you get caught in the snow," Red said. He shook his head. "Just not worth it. So, people stay here, where at least we have knights and a warning signal."

I tried to push the discussion of dragons out of my head for the rest of the morning, but a gnawing feeling told me that Drake wasn't safe in Trulith.

Chapter 19

Needing time to think about whether to stay in Trulith or pack up my family and look for somewhere safer to live, I took a longer path home from work that day. Even if Drake had to stay hidden wherever we lived, he'd be much safer in an area that didn't have its citizens already in an uproar against dragons. Maybe in time, I could save enough money to buy what we'd need to go back home and fix up our old place. Drake had been happy and safe there...well, until the men showed up.

Would any place be safe for him?

When I entered the house, Nyla said, "The boys are out," without looking up from her work at the table. She was involved in another embroidery project. "There's some soup on the stove if you're hungry."

"Thanks," I said as I hung my coat. I rubbed my hands together to warm them.

Kate and Dora lay on their bellies near the fireplace, their feet sticking up behind them.

"Look, Zander," Kate said with a smile. "I'm teaching Dora to draw."

I stood over them and tilted my head to see. "That's a pretty picture, Dora," I said.

"Can you tell what it is?" Dora asked, and I cringed inwardly.

Kate must have sensed the reason for my hesitation. She lightly bumped Dora's shoulder. "Of course he can. That looks just like a horse we used to have."

A horse? Um, okay. "Yes, that's a good-looking horse," I said, winking at Kate. I glanced at Kate's picture and saw a drawing of Drake. I quickly pulled the paper from the floor.

"Hey," Kate said as she jumped up, trying to take it from my hands.

I put my finger to my lips to shush her. I raised my eyebrows as I folded the paper and put it in my pocket. "This one is so good, I'm going to keep it."

She noticed my pointed look, and her eyes grew wide when she realized what she'd done. I gave her shoulder a quick squeeze.

"Nyla?" I called.

"Mmm-hmm," she responded mindlessly, focusing on her stitching.

"What do you know about a man named Marlon?"

She stopped what she was doing and looked up as I sat next to her at the table. "Marlon?" She scrunched up her face. "With the black hair, always wearing a long coat?"

"That's the one."

She lowered her project. "I don't know a lot about him, just things I've heard, but he's in a bad situation. He tried to protect his family during the very first dragon attack on Trulith but ended up getting seriously injured with a claw mark down the side of his face. His father and sister died when a building collapsed on them. He only has his mother left, but she suffered a bad blow to the head during the attack." Nyla frowned. "She hasn't been right ever since. Oh, and once when he was out hunting dragons,

I heard there was a fire, and he suffered burns all along one side of his body."

Long dark coat. Dragon hunting. A fire. Kate and I exchanged a quick glance. Her mouth fell open when she realized what I had already thought was true.

"That's terrible," I said.

"Why do you ask?"

"Kate and I saw him several days ago outside the tavern, and I just had a run-in with him at the stable. He's a very unpleasant man." Seeing the concern on Kate's face, I changed the subject. "So, there's soup?"

Nyla nodded.

"Do you want some, Kate?" I called as I ladled the soup into a bowl for myself.

"No, I already ate."

I sat down at the table and sighed. "Ugh, a spoon," I said as I moved to get up.

"I'll get it for you," Kate said. As she came near the table, she glanced at Nyla's stitching. "Oh, that's so pretty. What's it for?"

"I get orders from people for embroidered designs on towels and handkerchiefs. I haven't been doing it for very long, but I enjoy it, and it brings in some extra coin."

I looked at the needlework for the first time and noticed detailed flowers and colorful butterflies. I'd never seen anything like it.

Kate sat next to me, handing me the spoon. "What do you do with the money you make?" she asked Nyla.

I shoveled the soup into my mouth, enjoying the warmth as it slid down my throat.

"I use it to buy things we need here. With my healing work,

people sometimes pay me a little bit, but I also have to buy the bandages and supplies. I won't steal things like the boys used to do. I tried it once a long time ago and got caught."

I turned toward her. "What happened?"

She paused a moment as her eyes fell to the table. She shook her head as she spoke. "I was foolish. I'd seen a kid take something just by grabbing it and putting it in his pocket. It looked so easy, and he got away with it. Nobody had even looked at him. I was so hungry. Dora and I hadn't eaten in two days, so I went into a bakery and took some bread, hoping it would get us through a couple of days." She chuckled as she looked at me. "I hadn't realized that I had nowhere to hide this ridiculously long loaf of bread. I tried to hide it in my buttoned jacket, but it stuck out of the top as if I had a second head. Like I said, I was foolish." Her smile faded as she went back to her embroidery. "It was the first and last time I ever stole anything."

"What happened when you got caught?" Kate asked timidly.

Nyla turned and lifted the back of her tunic just enough to show three long scars across her back.

Kate drew in a sharp breath. "They whipped you?"

Nyla lowered her clothing and nodded. "I suppose it's good that it was a long time ago, since the king now deals out harsher, more obvious punishments for stealing. That's what started my interest in healing. The woman who took care of my back told me every step of what she was doing. I asked questions, and she was happy to teach me."

"How did you end up with Red and Luca?" I asked.

"About two years ago, Dora and I had been living on the streets for a few weeks, but not doing it very well. We'd been surviving on handouts from shopkeepers or raiding their discards after they closed each evening. One day, from a distance, I saw Red take something from a store and pass it to Luca to hide for him. Then Red took something else and kept it for himself. The two looked like experts at what they were doing. Not a single adult took notice of them.

"I was intrigued, so Dora and I followed them, and they ended up here. Somehow, I found the courage to talk to them and eventually asked if we could live with them. We made an arrangement that they would provide the food, and I would cook it. My momma was a good cook and taught me before she passed." Nyla paused. She cleared her throat. "Anyway, I also offered to mend their clothes. They had ratty holes all over them. I could do all the things a momma normally did to keep a household running. And I could take care of their injuries with my knowledge of healing. Back then, they were always coming back with scratches and scrapes. They also watched Dora for me when I'd need to go out sometimes. It was good that we ended up together. We all provided something the others needed. It's a blessing to have someone looking out for you, you know?" She returned her focus to her embroidery.

I smiled at Kate, and she nodded. We knew exactly what she meant.

Chapter 20

One morning when I didn't have to work, Kate and I slipped out just as the sun started to rise. Taking Buddy with us, we quietly made our way through the streets of the city and out to the meadow. Buddy was the first to reach Drake, and the dog and dragon played like they always did—chasing each other, with Buddy barking and Drake making his throaty growling noises. My heart lightened and Kate giggled as we watched them play. We sat together on our usual fallen log near the edge of the trees.

When he tired of playing, Drake came over and nudged Kate's arm, nearly knocking her from her seat. She laughed, and he laid down flat on his belly in front of her. She knelt beside him and wrapped her arms around his neck, while I rubbed his snout. The dragon closed his eyes, loving the attention. Kate pulled an apple from her pocket and laid it on the ground in front of him. As soon as he saw his favorite treat, his lips twitched upward into a slight smile—if dragons could actually smile. In one swift gulp, the apple disappeared.

Kate patted Drake's neck again. "You're welcome," she said sweetly.

"Look what I have." I pulled Buddy's favorite ball from my coat pocket. As soon as Buddy saw it, he barked repeatedly, and Drake let out a low rumble of pleasure. Chasing a ball was one of their favorite things to do, second only to chasing each other.

I threw the ball as far as I could. Buddy, being more agile than Drake, quickly turned and ran after the ball which had landed at the far end of the clearing. Drake, knowing he could be faster than his gravity-challenged friend if he chose to fly, shot a sideways glance at me. I grinned at the obvious head start he had granted the dog. Drake flapped his wings and became airborne. My hair ruffled from the breeze. He swooped low across the open area with only a few pumps of his wings. He landed a short distance ahead of Buddy, putting him closer to the ball. Instead of putting it in his mouth—which was how we had lost many balls over the years—he used his front leg to bat it away from Buddy. I laughed, realizing the game of fetch had now become a game of keep-away.

Kate leaned against me and gave a contented sigh as we watched Drake and Buddy play. I smiled, feeling the same way she did. Things weren't perfect in our new life, but they were going much better than I expected.

Just when I thought Kate had dozed off, she sat up quickly, her eyebrows furrowed together.

"What is it?" I asked as I looked around.

She put a finger to her lips for silence and then pointed to her ear and over her shoulder. My heart skipped a beat at the sound of a twig snapping and the soft crunch of leaves. Kate looked at me, her face filled with alarm.

I immediately shouted "Drake, hide!" Within seconds, both dog and dragon had hidden themselves behind the trees at the other side of the clearing. I jumped up from the log and pushed Kate to stand behind me.

A split-second later, there was a loud rustling as something burst through the tall bushes that bordered the meadow. Kate and I jumped. I'd expected an animal, but it was a person. And I would recognize that long coat, black hat, and stringy hair anywhere.

"Marlon," I muttered under my breath. "What do you want?"

"*I'll* be asking the questions around here." He glared at me with his one uncovered eye. Marlon shifted his focus from me to the spot where Drake and Buddy had just been playing. He frowned. "Where did they go? I know they were here. I saw them!"

"Saw who?" I kept my voice steady, despite my pounding heart. Here I was, standing face-to-face with the man who might have been responsible for my father's death. A storm of emotions swirled inside me. I was angry, yes, but there was also a twinge of fear. Part of me wanted to run away, but my family needed me to protect them.

Marlon stepped over the log to stand in front of us. He raised his long thin arm and pointed toward Drake's last location. "The dog and that dragon. I saw them!"

I made a show of looking in that direction and felt relieved there was no sign of them. I shrugged. "There's nothing over there," I said calmly before looking back at our accuser.

Marlon sighed and looked there again. "I saw them!" He pointed his finger with each word.

"Yes, you keep saying that."

"I know what I saw." Marlon's lips formed a tight line. He clenched his fists and limped across the clearing, his long coat billowing behind him.

Kate gave me a worried look. We ran to catch up. Unfortunately, even with his limp, Marlon's long legs made him much faster, and he reached the edge of the clearing before we did. As soon as he drew near, Buddy came out of the forest, hackles raised, baring his teeth as he gave his most menacing growl. Marlon jumped back, let out a yell, and instantly threw his hands up in front of him. Buddy continued to snarl, taking small but certain steps toward the threat. It was then that I remembered that Buddy had bitten one of the strangers at the barn. Marlon must be that man!

I watched closely, ready to call off the dog if needed. But I knew Buddy was only protecting his hidden friend, who I hoped had enough sense to remain out of sight. If Marlon ever got a good look at Drake, everything in our lives would change.

A sudden gust of wind caused the trees to sway. The dead leaves on the ground swirled. That same breeze lifted Marlon's hat, which he caught in mid-air, but not before his hair moved out of place, fully exposing his face. Kate gasped when she saw the scars covering the left side of it. The skin was puckered and shiny from burns. Two jagged cuts had made parallel lines through his pale skin, leaving red scars. I could only imagine how painful that must have been, and how painful it must be even now.

Before I could stop her, Kate blurted, "What happened to your face?"

Marlon turned to us, scowling, as he swept his hair over his wounded eye and tugged his hat on. I pulled Kate closer to me.

"Dragon," he sneered, leaning toward her. "Dragons are despicable beings, deserving only death. Every single one! And mark my words, that's exactly what I will make happen."

Kate took a breath to say something, so I put my hand over her mouth. Buddy continued barking, and I decided right then that I wouldn't stop the dog if he moved to attack. We needed Buddy to fill this man with fear so he'd leave.

I stood straight and tall, looking Marlon in the eye. "There is nothing here for you. You should go. You've already upset my sister and my dog. Leave now, or I'll give my dog the order to attack you."

Buddy growled, baring his teeth. Perfect timing. He took two steps closer and barked again.

Marlon stepped further back, clearly terrified of the dog. He pointed his finger in my face. "I'll be watching you. And if I see that dragon again, I'll tell the king's army, or I'll kill it myself and collect the reward." He turned so quickly, the bottom of his coat slapped my legs.

As he walked across the meadow, I yelled, "Buddy, get him!" and the dog zoomed over the dead grass. Marlon heard him coming and ran limping into the trees.

When Buddy reached the tree line, I called, "Buddy, stay!"

The dog stopped running but continued barking and growling. If Marlon were smart, he'd keep running and never look back.

"Buddy, come!" I called, and he ran back to us, his tongue lolling out to the side. He didn't need to be able to speak; it was obvious what he felt—pride in protecting his family. Kate and I heaped praise and attention on our brave dog.

"I don't like that man," Kate said.

Trying to sound reassuring, I said, "Don't you worry. He isn't going to hurt Drake."

"But he's the man we saw that day by the butcher shop. He's mean."

She didn't know the half of it.

I crouched down in front of her. "We can either worry about him every day, or we can do what we can to keep our family safe.

What do you think we should do?"

"Choose joy," she said with a determination I admired.

"We have a huge forest here. Let's move Drake's nest deeper into the woods, just in case Marlon decides to come looking for him again."

Kate agreed with the plan.

After a few moments, the ball rolled out from among the trees, stopping when it hit my boot. A laugh spurted out of me, and I looked across the clearing to be sure it was safe. I gave a soft whistle, and Drake's head popped out from the trees.

"It's all right," Kate said sweetly as she walked to him. "The bad man is gone. You can come out now."

She backed up a few steps as Drake slowly emerged from his hiding spot. He looked all around the clearing.

"He's scared, Zander."

I just nodded in response. Yes, Drake was scared. He must have recognized Marlon.

What exactly happened in our barn? If only Drake could talk.

Chapter 21

"What's in the bag?" Kate asked innocently.

"Enough with the questions." I rolled my eyes in mock frustration as I heaved a long drawstring bag onto my shoulder. "I've told you that today is a surprise. The whole day. So keep your questions to yourself because I'm not going to answer them."

Kate pretended to be annoyed.

Nyla leaned toward her as she held dirty breakfast dishes in her hands. "You're lucky to have a brother who cares about you so much. You get to do something fun while I'm stuck here." She made a silly face before going to the kitchen counter.

I knew what Kate was about to say but was unable to stop her in time. "You can go with us if you want, Nyla—you and Dora. Can't they, Zander?"

I opened my mouth to answer her, but Nyla took care of the problem for me.

"Aw, thank you, but we can't. I have two embroidery pieces for Lady Mary that I must finish today." Nyla glanced at me and gave me a quick smile as she handed me the bag of sandwiches I'd packed earlier. "You two go and have fun."

I was eager to enjoy a day off. My days kept me busy, and Kate and I had fallen into our routine. My mornings were filled working at the stable while Kate helped Nyla and Dora with chores around the house. Most afternoons, Kate and I made time to sneak out and visit Drake deep in the woods. Other afternoons, I usually worked special clean-up jobs for Antony or helped Red and Luca with projects they couldn't do alone. Word had spread about our reliability, so sometimes we were asked to do work for local merchants, repairing items or moving new stock from a wagon into a store. I was happy to do it since I'd get paid. Most evenings were spent quietly in front of the fire, where I'd whittle while Kate drew or learned embroidery from Nyla. I felt true contentment here in Trulith. It had turned out to be everything I'd hoped, except for the nagging worry about Drake's safety.

The previous day, Antony had given me permission to borrow a horse from the castle stable. Kate loved visiting the horses, but that only happened if Nyla had business in the castle and brought her along. I had told Red earlier about my plan for an outing, so he had a horse named Ranger saddled and ready for us when we arrived. Buddy came into the stable with Kate and waited by her side.

I filled the brown horse's saddlebags with our food and water. Red helped me tie the drawstring bag along the side of the horse, since it was too long to put anywhere else.

"That guy was in here earlier," Red said, tipping his head toward Midnight's empty stall.

A chill ran down my spine. "Who? Marlon?"

"Yeah. Came in looking mad at the world. Mumbled something about following the soldiers this time because 'they don't know what they're doing.'" Red sighed. "I really hate the way he treats his horse."

I glanced at Kate and saw the look of concern on her face. I was just about to change the subject when Binobrik, the gardener, did it for me.

He stopped shoveling manure into a bucket and smiled. "I see you're embarking on an adventure, Mister Zander. I once went on a grand adventure myself."

"Oh? How was it?" I asked while Red guided the horse out of the stall. He held the reins while I lifted Kate onto the front edge of the saddle.

"It was a jollywomp until I got separated from my friends and was sucked down a fast-flowing river." The gnome shrugged. "Nearly drowned. I'm certain I would have died if Sir Antony hadn't found me."

"Did you ever find your friends?" Kate asked.

"Unfortunately, no. I couldn't have found them if I tried. The river took me a long way from them. Nope, no more adventures for me. I'm staying put. The dragons here are enough of an adventure. Besides, the flowers need me." He pointed to the bucket. "The horses provide the perfect ingredient to improve the dirt."

I took the reins from Red and mounted the horse, sitting directly behind Kate. "Ready?"

"Ready!" she said, her voice high with excitement.

"Have fun!" Red called.

"Stay away from fast-moving water!" Binobrik said with a wave.

"Bye, Binobrik Fizzlewhistle!" called Kate. She whispered to me, "I like saying his name. It's fun. But what's a jollywomp?"

"I have no idea."

I gently nudged Ranger forward. It had been a while since I'd ridden, but it came back to me quickly. With Kate between my arms, she melted into me, relaxing as we left the stone walls of the city. Buddy happily jogged alongside us, also eager for this adventure.

"Let's go fast, Zander!"

I pushed my heels into Ranger's sides and yelled, "Hyah!" The horse immediately responded, and Kate squealed. Buddy, unaware of what was going on, was left behind but yipped and did his best to catch up. We didn't slow until we reached Drake's woods.

Kate giggled. "That was fun!" she said, clapping her hands.

When we reached the woods, I dismounted but left Kate in the saddle as I took the reins to lead Ranger through the trees. The fallen leaves crunched beneath my boots, followed by the horse's heavy hooves and Buddy's light, jaunty paws.

We had moved Drake's nest deeper into the woods, near a glade that wasn't quite as big as the other one. It meant more walking time for us, but it was worth it if it kept him safe. At the clearing, I called for Drake while Buddy ran ahead to find him. After I called a second time, Drake's head poked out of a full evergreen bush. Once he saw Buddy, he came out and did the usual tail-wag greeting they always shared. I could tell they were about to begin a game of chase, but we needed to be on our way.

"No, Buddy. No, Drake," I called as I waved them over to me. "Come." They responded immediately, with Drake happily running toward me on all fours just like the dog.

"Hi, Drake," Kate called with a wave.

As the dragon drew close to her, the horse showed its unease by taking a few steps back.

"Shhh, it's okay," I whispered calmly as I stroked Ranger's neck. "This is Drake. He's a friend."

I could tell the dragon wanted to get closer to Kate and the horse, but I held up my hand to stop him. "No, Drake. Stay back." And he did. Once again, the many hours I'd spent training both dog and dragon had paid off.

Leading the horse into the forest beyond the glade, I called for Buddy and Drake to follow. We hadn't been through this part of the woods before, although it looked just the same as the rest of it. There were still plenty of trees, fallen leaves, and small animals skittering around. Birds chirped from the tree limbs above, but most grew silent when Drake passed by. Even the birds knew this creature was not natural to their forest.

Drake would be a frightening sight to anyone. When he stood on his hind legs reaching his full height, he could be terrifying.

That, and the fire-breathing thing.

And the sharp teeth and talons.

I smiled to myself because Kate and I knew who Drake really was. Even though he could be dangerous—past actions had proved that—he was also playful and caring and brave. Those traits wouldn't typically come to mind if anyone else thought of a fire-breathing dragon. Would Drake have been that way if he hadn't been raised around humans and hadn't had a dog as a best friend? Who knew? But having Buddy with Drake these past several years certainly had brought out the fun side of the dragon. It was too bad the dragons attacking Trulith didn't have a dog to help them be kind and fun-loving. Maybe that was what every dragon needed—a dog for a best friend.

After pushing our way through the trees and brush, we came to a small clearing. Buddy darted out in front of me, yipping gleefully and running in circles. Drake was blocked behind the horse but caught up to Buddy as soon as he could. I helped Kate down so she could stretch her legs. We walked as I guided Ranger by his reins. Dog and dragon played in the distance but didn't stray too far.

Kate held my hand. "So," she said with a hint of playfulness in her voice, "where are we going?"

I chuckled. "You'd like for me to tell you, wouldn't you?"

Her face took on a serious look. "Yes, I would."

I leaned down and bonked her forehead with mine. "Nope. Not going to tell you...yet."

She sighed and tried to look frustrated, crossing her arms across her chest, but I caught the hint of a smile.

When we reached the outer edge of the woods, we mounted the horse once more. I guided Ranger along groupings of trees as often as possible, knowing Drake's green body would camouflage well against the evergreens. While I didn't expect to see anyone, I still had to be careful.

We rode for about a half-hour at a pace slow enough for Buddy to keep up. I found the area Nial had told me about, a large meadow surrounded by huge trees and far from people. It was at the base of a steep mountain with no signs of homesteads or a village. Freedom to be ourselves was my hope for this day—for Drake most of all.

After dismounting, Kate stretched and yawned, then patted her rumbling stomach. "I'm hungry. When can we eat?"

"Right now. This is where we're spending the afternoon." I pulled the supplies from the saddlebags and found a rock-free spot to have our picnic lunch. Buddy and Drake wandered off to explore the area together.

"We get to spend the whole afternoon here?" Kate's eyes sparkled with joy as she helped me spread out the blanket. The wind had picked up, whipping the blanket around as we fought to lay it on the ground.

"That's the plan. Just a day to relax and be together with Buddy and Drake."

"And no one else," she said with a big grin as she sat on the blanket.

"And no one else."

I set out our food, and Kate pretended to be at a formal luncheon. Realizing she needed a chance to behave like any little girl her age, I joined in on the display of prim and proper manners. I held out my pinkie finger as I drank, and Kate fell over from laughing so hard. I enjoyed watching her have so much fun. Even if nothing else came from our outing, this chance to be silly with her was worth it all.

Toward the end of the meal, Buddy quietly came to the edge of the blanket, sniffing for leftovers.

"Oh, poor Buddy," Kate said as she stroked his head. "No food for you."

I lifted a finger. "Oh, but there is," I said as I went to the saddlebags.

I pulled out a paper-wrapped package, and Buddy's nose immediately started wiggling as he sniffed the air with interest. Unwrapping the bundle revealed two large meat bones. Buddy yipped with glee. I let him smell one before I threw it across the clearing. He ran for it, his tail wagging in circles.

Not wanting to miss out on anything, Drake came to us, his nostrils wiggling, too.

I patted his neck. "I didn't forget you. It's small for you, so try to make it last."

I threw his bone and watched as Drake chased after it. The

dragon grabbed it, and they lay on the grass, side by side, enjoying their rare treat.

Once lunch was cleared, I untied the long drawstring bag from Ranger. Kate rose up on her knees and clapped excitedly. "I've been wondering what that is. Are you going to tell me now?"

"No," I said with a smile. "I'm going to *show* you." I joined her on the blanket and carefully removed each piece from the bag.

She watched intently. "What is this?"

"Just wait. Hmm, let me see if I can figure out how this goes together."

I studied the pieces as I tried to remember the toy maker's instructions. I laid out the yellow diamond-shaped cloth on the blanket, put the two sticks together in a "t" formation, tied the twine around it to hold it in place, and inserted the corners of the cloth into the slits on the ends of the wooden sticks.

"What's this for?" Kate asked, lifting a long strip of green fabric. "I like this color," she said cheerfully. "It reminds me of the grass at home in the summertime."

She handed me the strip of cloth, which I tied to the bottom of it. Holding the shape's sticks in one hand and the remaining ball of twine in the other, I stood up. "Ta-daaa!" I sang proudly as I showed her the finished product.

She clapped excitedly. "That's beautiful, Zander." She squinted one eye shut as she studied it. "What is it?"

I laughed. "It's called a kite, and the toy maker said it's best used on a windy day. He told me how to make it fly, but I'll need your help."

"Okay," she said jumping up. "What do I do?"

I loved how she was always ready for an adventure.

We walked to the middle of the meadow. I gave her the kite,

placing her hands on opposite ends of the horizontal stick. "Now stand here and hold it while I walk out there. Then when I tell you to, toss it up into the air, and it'll fly."

"This will fly?" she said skeptically as she studied it. "It doesn't have wings. How's it going to fly?"

"Just watch. I've never done this before, so it might take a few tries."

After making sure that she had a good grip on the kite, I carefully unwound the twine and stepped away, continuing to unroll it as I walked. When I was a good distance from her, I called out, "Throw it toward the sky like you're throwing a ball up above your head."

She did as I told her, and the wind caught the kite, lifting it into the sky. Kate squealed and ran to me. Buddy and Drake came to see what was causing her excitement. I let out the string a little bit at a time, just like the toy maker had told me. Moments later, Drake entered my view, lazily flapping his wings as he circled the kite, careful to avoid the string. I kept the kite fairly low so Drake could stay near it.

"He thinks it's a bird," Kate giggled. She cupped her hands around her mouth and called, "Drake, it's a kite, not a bird!"

Buddy yipped as he stood near Kate, who had returned to sit on the picnic blanket.

After a while, I walked toward her. "My turn?" she asked.

Sitting down next to her, I handed her the ball of twine. I gave her some instructions and watched as she held the string in both hands, keeping her eyes on the kite. Drake continued to fly around in the clearing, happy to stretch his wings and be above ground level. Soon, Buddy joined in the fun by running beneath Drake, barking joyfully at his airborne friend.

We'd been having so much fun, I failed to notice the sky growing cloudy. The wind increased, turning colder, and it smelled of rain. That meant it was time to go home. Despite Kate's whining, I quickly dismantled the kite, shoved it in the bag, and loaded everything onto Ranger as I called to Drake and Buddy.

Our day of fun was over. Now I had to focus on beating that storm.

Chapter 22

The wind pushed against us more strongly than I had ever experienced. The frigid air stole my breath as I urged the horse forward to Drake's meadow. Overhead, clouds formed like a thick, dark blanket, ready to smother us with rain. Thunder rumbled, echoing all around us. The darkening sky looked like nighttime had come early. The gathering storm mirrored the storm of worry swirling inside me.

I urged Ranger to go faster. Buddy and Drake followed close behind.

The chill seeped through my coat. I pulled my hood over my head and did the same for Kate as she leaned her back into me, seeking warmth.

As soon as we reached the edge of Drake's forest, the first raindrop landed on my hand.

"Ohhh," Kate whined. "I wanted it to wait until we got home."

I jumped off the horse and walked Ranger quickly through the crowded trees. When we arrived at the clearing, I patted Drake's neck.

"Okay, you're home now. Try to stay dry."

He gently put his forehead against mine and then hurried to his favorite edge of the forest.

When I swung around to mount the horse, Kate wasn't in the saddle. She had slipped off by herself.

"Drake, wait!" she called as she ran to catch up to him.

"Kate, come back! We don't have time!" I yelled through cupped hands, but a crash of thunder muffled my voice. A flicker of lightning just above the trees caught my attention. "Oh, no," I muttered to myself. "Now we *really* have to go."

As she ran, Kate shouted over her shoulder, "I need to say goodbye to Drake!"

She'd barely said the words when the air crackled just before a blinding light flashed in the darkness. The force threw me to the shaking ground as a boom echoed all around. The hair on my arms sprang up. Ranger whinnied in fright. I blinked hard, trying to make my eyes see through white spots in my vision.

Once I caught my breath, I stood slowly, fighting against my shaking legs. A cough rattled from deep inside my chest.

Just then, the clouds opened up and the rain poured down.

Where was Kate? She was nowhere to be seen. She seemed to have vanished behind the curtain of water.

Drake let out a loud bellow. I ran toward the sound. Squinting against the rain pelting my face, I caught a glimpse of him standing on his hind legs, carrying a limp Kate in his arms. Her head lolled to the side, eyes closed. Steam rose around the two of them.

"No, no. Please, no!" I said under my breath as I ran to Drake. "Kate! Kate!" I screamed, lifting her from the dragon's arms. I laid her on the soggy ground and shook her. "Kate! Wake up!" Her chest barely rose and fell from her breaths. I slapped her face lightly to wake her, but there was no change. "What do I do? I don't know what to do!" I said to nobody.

Suddenly, the rain stopped falling on us, even though it continued to pour nearby. I looked up and saw that Drake had stretched his wings over us just enough to shield us from the rain. A horrible keening sound came from him. It expressed exactly how I felt.

Smoke rose from the front of her coat and a burning odor met my nose. Strands of Kate's brown hair had escaped from her hood and had separated into individual strands, now hanging weightlessly in the air. Finally, she let out several deep coughs. My relief was short-lived, though; she opened her eyes, but they seemed lifeless—just staring into nothing.

"Kate, can you hear me?" I asked, leaning over her, shaking her shoulders. My whole body trembled as she looked toward me with unfocused eyes. "Kate! I'll take you home. Nyla can help."

Again, a blank stare. I fought the panic pushing its way through me. At least she was breathing and alive.

As I began to stand, Drake gently picked her up. I ran to Ranger, grabbed the reins, and jumped onto the saddle. I uttered calming sounds and patted the horse's neck as he shied from Drake's approach.

The dragon placed Kate's limp body into my outstretched arms. When his arm touched mine, he looked into my eyes, and everything seemed to stop for a moment. My mind saw a scene of Drake and Kate being hit by lightning at the same time. I saw her fall to the ground while Drake stood nearby with smoke rising from his back. Then the scene jumped to me holding Kate on Ranger as the horse zoomed across the land toward the city gate.

My mouth fell open when the vision disappeared. I shook my head to get back to the present.

Drake moaned and gently rubbed his snout against Kate's arm

before stepping back. He loved her. That was very clear.

I repositioned her in front of me, pinning her in place with my arms. I called out for Buddy to follow, then guided Ranger through the maze of trees. It was frustratingly slow.

As soon as we made it out of the forest, I tightened my grip on Kate and commanded the horse into a full gallop, just like the vision had shown. Each time lightning flashed, I jumped, deathly afraid for our safety. I paid no attention as to whether Buddy kept up or not. The dog would find his way back to the house eventually. I couldn't wait for him.

Running the horse through the open gate of the city wall, I was relieved that most of the people had gone indoors, allowing me to get to the far edge of town quickly. I rode the horse right up to our door.

"Nyla!" I screamed, hoping to be heard over the thunder and rain. "Nyla!" The door opened. "Take her!" I cried.

"What happened?" she asked as I carefully slid Kate into her waiting arms.

"Lightning," was all I said as I followed her inside.

Drake carried Kate in his arms.

Chapter 23

Nyla immediately went into healer mode. "Luca, hurry. Take their horse to the stable."

"What happened?" he asked, jumping up from his chair. "Is she alive?"

"Yes, but barely," I replied, my voice cracking.

Luca threw on his coat and slammed the door in his haste to leave. Red immediately cleared the table, and we laid Kate's unmoving body on top of it. Dora cried out when she saw her friend.

"Tell me exactly what happened," Nyla said as she lifted Kate's arm a few inches off the table and let go. It flopped down with a thud.

With a shaking voice, I told her about the storm, carefully leaving out all references of Drake. When I mentioned the lightning, my eyes filled with tears as I thought about how irresponsible I'd been. It was careless of me not to notice the sky growing darker and the wind picking up. And now Kate might die because of me! It was my job to protect her, and I failed.

I wiped my tears and leaned into Kate's line of vision. "Hey, pretty girl, I'm right here," I said, trying to hide the quiver in my voice. Her eyes were open, and she blinked, but there was no acknowledgment that she heard or saw me. Tears ran down my cheeks again. I held her cold hand in both of mine. "Kate, please, please, be okay. I need you here with me." I kissed the back of her hand, and that was when I noticed strange red lines on her hand and wrist. "Nyla, look. What is this?"

Her eyes narrowed as she studied the marks. She pulled Kate's coat sleeve up and saw that the lines continued upward. "Help me take off her coat. But be careful. She might be hurting and unable to tell us."

Dora moaned, "Don't hurt her."

I helped Nyla remove the coat and scarf, leaving Kate only wearing her short-sleeved dress. I dropped the outerwear to the floor, and Dora immediately picked them up and tenderly placed them on the hook where they belonged.

Now that Kate's arms were exposed, we saw the red lines continuing up to her sleeves. "It looks like a vine with buds sprouting out of it," I said. I'd never seen anything like it. "What does that mean? What do we do?"

Nyla closed her eyes and rubbed her temples as she thought.

"The markings should go away in time." She nodded her head, as if confirming her own thoughts. She looked at me with confidence. "It's from the blood vessels just beneath the skin. They'll disappear on their own."

Kate shivered on the table and groaned softly, her head turning to the side. Her eyes closed and her body went limp again.

"Red," Nyla said, "build up a big fire. We need to keep her comfortable."

Red sprang into action and soon had a roaring fire heating up the room.

"So, what do we do now?" I asked when Nyla had finished examining Kate.

She shook her head. "I don't know. Let's cover her with some blankets and move the table closer to the fire."

After Red and I carefully moved the table, Dora held out Kate's pillow and doll to me. "She'll feel better with these," she said.

As I took the items from her, I bent down to her eye level. "Thank you, Dora. You are a good friend." Dora's smile lit up her whole face.

"I'll be back as soon as I can," Nyla said, getting into her coat and scarf.

"Where are you going? You can't leave us." I didn't even try to hide the panic in my voice.

"There's someone I need to talk to who might have some experience with this. Just keep her comfortable, and talk to her so she won't feel alone."

The minutes Nyla was gone felt like an eternity. I sat on the edge of the table next to Kate and did my best to talk to her. When I could no longer talk through my tears, I softly hummed some familiar songs instead, rubbing her arm so she would feel my touch. Red and Dora sat quietly nearby.

When Luca returned from the stable, Buddy came in with him. A blast of cold air pushed into the house.

"Buddy was waiting outside the door," Luca said, hanging his coat. He rubbed his hands together as he stood beside the table. "Will she be okay?" he asked, his face full of concern.

I just shrugged helplessly. He gently squeezed my shoulder and then moved toward the fire to warm his hands.

Buddy came to the table, put his front paws on it, and studied Kate. He let out a whine and licked her hand. My eyes again filled with tears. I rubbed the dog's wet head. Buddy lay down at my feet with a troubled sigh.

Moments later, Nyla came through the door. I jumped up. "Did you learn anything?" I asked expectantly.

She nodded as she threw her coat and scarf on a peg and came to the table. "Any change?"

I shook my head. "Nothing." My voice cracked.

"The healer said that she dealt with this type of injury only once before. Her patient also didn't respond at first but, after a day or so, he finally spoke. We just need to give her time." Nyla gently held one of Kate's hands, rubbing her thumb over the little knuckles. "The thing is that the lightning affected this man's hearing and sight for a while. His hearing was completely gone for a day or two but gradually improved." She hesitated for a moment and looked up at me. "But he completely lost sight in one eye."

My heart dropped as I realized Kate's life could be changed forever. This was all my fault. It had been my job to keep her safe.

Nyla reached across the table and touched my arm. "You need to trust that everything's going to work out. We don't know if she can hear us or not, so talk to her. She may not be able to see you, but hearing your voice or feeling your touch may calm her."

"We can help with that, too," Red said, pointing to him and Luca.

"We'll do whatever you need," Luca said, putting a hand on my shoulder. "Anything to help."

"I can sing to her," Dora offered.

"Thank you," I whispered, as I looked at each of them—this family we had become. "Thank you so much."

Buddy sat up and put his paw on my leg. I scratched his head.

"It's okay, Buddy. She'll be okay."
  Maybe if I kept saying that, it would come true.

Chapter 24

The next day passed with no noticeable improvement. Red and Luca worked in the stable that morning, insisting that I stay home with Kate. When they returned, Red said the stable master told me to take as much time as I needed. One less worry was a welcome change.

That evening, Nyla made stew and bread which we ate near the fire. We had backed the table away from the fireplace, since the blankets seemed to be keeping Kate warm enough. Buddy had kept a constant watch beside the table. As we ate, he raised his head and whined, looking at me.

That's when I saw it: her hand wasn't where it had been before. "I think she moved!" I hurried to the table, followed by Nyla. The others gathered around and watched Kate expectantly. Buddy whined louder, and at almost the same time, Kate moved her head and moaned softly.

I held her hand and leaned in. "Hey, Kate. I'm right here."

Nyla lifted Kate's arm and checked her pulse. "Stronger than yesterday." She gave me an encouraging smile.

A tear of relief slipped down my cheek. We had no idea how bad her injuries were, but at least now there was progress in her healing.

Buddy and I stayed by her side the rest of the evening. When I could no longer keep my eyes open, I lay down on the floor next to the table. Buddy curled up next to me, resting his head on my arm. Nyla covered me with a blanket and lowered the flame on the nearby lamp.

Bad dreams of lightning and death filled my troubled sleep, causing me to jerk awake over and over again.

A hand on my arm shook me awake. I blinked, and my breath quickened as I tried to remember where I was.

Luca lowered his face to mine. "My friend, that was quite a dream you had. You were moaning and yelling."

I rubbed my face and sat up. Buddy moved closer and laid his head on my lap.

"Are you okay?" Luca asked.

I nodded. "Sorry I woke you."

He squeezed my shoulders with both hands. "Hey, you've been through a lot. It's okay."

"I keep having nightmares about the storm."

"Is there anything I can do?"

I shook my head.

He patted my shoulder. "Then try to get some sleep."

He returned to the bedroom, quietly closing the door. I lowered myself to the floor, and Buddy nestled in beside me. Laying my arm over him, I mindlessly rubbed his fur until sleep overtook me.

Kate had no more visible improvements until later the next morning. As the day dragged on, her slight movements caused an eruption of excitement from anyone near enough to notice. Finally, she coughed and groaned, moving her mouth as if trying to speak. She followed me with her eyes but didn't turn her head to see anything out of her range of vision. We all continued to talk to her, whether close by her side or across the room, hoping she could hear us.

Early on the third morning, Kate rubbed her eyes. I had fallen asleep with my arms cushioning my head on the table, but the sound of her movement woke me.

"Nyla!" I called. "She rubbed her eyes!" I told her as she quickly came out of the bedroom. Kate blinked hard. "Hey, Kate," I whispered, swallowing the lump in my throat. I stroked her tangled hair. She turned her head toward me and looked at me for a long time. The corners of her mouth turned up in a slight smile. "She knows me! She recognizes me!" I wanted to shout it from the rooftop for all to hear! I leaned over and kissed her forehead. "Don't be afraid. Things might feel a bit strange for a while, but you're going to be all right."

Nyla brought her a cup of water and helped her sit up to drink. When we laid her back down, Dora came to the table.

"Hi, Kate," she whispered, tears filling her eyes. "I'm glad you're better."

Kate smiled, then closed her eyes and slept.

Sitting on a chair beside the table, I rested my elbows on my knees and let my head drop as I stared at the floor.

Nyla touched my shoulder. I looked up and she said in a motherly tone, "You need to climb into your bed and get some real sleep."

"I need to stay here to make sure she's okay." My voice cracked. I cleared my throat. "She's my responsibility." I whispered to myself, "I failed her."

Nyla's skirt swished as she knelt in front of me. "No, Zander, you did not fail her. It was just an accident. You've been doing a wonderful job taking care of her—and keeping your family together. Your parents would be so proud." She patted my hand. "Now go to bed and get some sleep. I'll wake you if there's any change."

I did as she said, although I lay in bed and stared at the ceiling for a long time. I replayed Nyla's words in my head and let them soothe my worries, allowing me to finally drift off to sleep.

We moved Kate to her bed, so she could rest more comfortably. Her recovery was slow but steady over the next few days. Soon, it felt like I had my Kate back. Her hearing had been affected by the lightning strike, but everyone made a special effort to talk more loudly around her and use their hands to help her understand their words. Thankfully, her eyesight was unharmed. Her speech was slow to return to normal, maybe because of the hearing impairment, but it didn't stop her from giggling any time Buddy licked her face or when I swung her around in a fast twirl. After all that time worrying if she would live through the ordeal, any bit of laughter was welcome.

One day when we were alone, I told her about how carefully Drake had picked her up and carried her to me.

She smiled and said, "I saw that."

"You what?"

She pointed to her forehead. "In here. When Drake carried me to you, he showed me when the lightning hit both of us. He showed me that he was taking me to you. And he told me he loved me. Then I went to sleep."

Was it possible? My mind reeled with the thought: Drake was struck by lightning, too, and since that moment, he'd somehow been able to share his thoughts with us by touch!

Kate wanted to visit Drake as soon as we could. A week after the lightning strike, we rode to the meadow. I watched her express her gratitude to the dragon in the way that only Kate could, and my eyes filled with tears.

I sniffed as I shoved my hands in my pockets, standing back to give them space. Drake looked at me and tilted his head. He walked over on all fours and slowly touched his forehead to mine. In that instant, I saw another vision. Now I understood. This was a message coming from Drake himself.

My mind pictured the inside of our barn, like I was floating in the air, watching everything happen. The two men in black coats ran into the barn yelling, one holding his sword out in front of him, and the other holding a large coil of rope. Drake sat up in his temporary nest as they entered, his eyes filled with confusion and fear as he looked from one man to the other. He limped as he backed up several steps, his hind foot bandaged from his previous injury. Drake bumped into the barn wall behind him. He turned to look, taking his eyes off the strangers for just a moment. The men chose that moment to charge at him. The man uncoiled the rope as he ran the length of the barn. He swung the circle of rope around and around above his head before letting it fly. It landed on Drake and settled around his neck. He flinched at the impact and tried to see what was on his neck just as the man pulled to tighten the rope. Drake's front foot tugged at the rope but couldn't release it. He swung his head from side to side trying to loosen it. The man with the sword ran toward him, aiming at Drake's belly. That's when the dragon took a deep breath and blasted out a stream of fire that instantly incinerated the sword-wielding attacker. At that same moment, Pa had run forward, partially hidden behind that man. The man with the rope moved far enough off to the side that he managed to miss most of the blast, but the barn was aflame instantly, and he screamed, running to find a way out. Drake crashed through the burning wall and ran into the forest.

The vision in my head went black as Drake stepped back. A tear streaked down his snout as his mournful eyes watched me.

For the first time, I knew for certain that Drake hadn't seen Pa behind the man when he breathed the fire. They loved each other, and Drake wouldn't have hurt him on purpose. Come to think of it, Drake wouldn't have been resting in the barn that day if *I* hadn't caused his injury in the first place. A shiver ran through me as I fully understood the horrifying part I played in that terrible event.

"Drake, I..." I didn't even know how to start. Choking back a sob, I hugged his neck. My heart demanded to be unburdened. "I know you won't understand what I'm saying, but I need to apologize. I blamed you for Pa's death, and I had a hard time seeing past that for a long time. You wouldn't have even been in the barn if you hadn't gotten injured while I was training you. I know you would never intentionally hurt one of us." I smiled gently. "We're family, and we don't do that to each other. For all of it, I am so, so sorry." Tears streamed down my cheeks, and Drake let out a mournful moan.

Kate stared at me. She'd heard everything.

"I'm sorry," I said to her. I wiped my tears with my sleeves. "I should have told you before now."

"I already knew. I'm sad that it took you so long to make up with Drake, but it's good that you finally did."

"You knew? You knew it was Drake that set the barn on fire? But you never said anything."

Her expression softened. "Zander, everyone makes mistakes. And like you said, family doesn't hurt each other. And Drake is family. I didn't want to blame him. I decided to choose joy." She squeezed my hand. "It's time for you to forgive yourself and choose joy, too."

Chapter 25

Our afternoon visits to see Drake became a priority for us, even when the bitterly cold wind took our breath away. Buddy happily joined us, eager for the chance to run and play.

On one visit, Drake and Buddy chased each other until exhaustion set in. Buddy plodded to the log at the edge of the clearing where I sat, the dog's tongue hanging out as he panted. Kate sat on a log on the other side of the clearing near the edge of the trees, contentedly drawing on paper she'd brought with her. She was probably making a picture of Drake, since no one was there to see it.

The dragon lay down near Buddy and me for only a short while before his attention was caught by a butterfly. It floated around the nearby wildflowers and then drew near to him. When it landed on his front foot, Drake lay perfectly still.

I looked across the meadow and noticed Kate frowning as she watched. No doubt she remembered what happened the last time a butterfly crossed paths with Drake.

The insect lazily opened and closed its wings as it rested on Drake's foot. He turned his head ever so slightly to look at Kate. Then he shook his foot just enough to make the butterfly take flight. Drake looked at me, slowly blinking as if to tell me that he'd learned his lesson the last time.

    I chuckled. When I looked over at Kate to make sure she'd seen Drake's good behavior, a movement in the bushes behind her caught my eye. A chill ran down my spine when the familiar black coat and hat came into view.

    "Kate!" I shouted. A look of confusion crossed her face. "Run!" I ran toward her, waving for her to come to me.

    Buddy barked and passed me in a white blur. Glancing over my shoulder, I noticed Drake had disappeared into the trees.

    Marlon grabbed Kate and lifted her off the ground, the familiar coiled rope now swinging from his belt. She screamed and kicked, her little body writhing in his clutches. He put an arm across the front of her. My heart dropped as an eerie smile crossed his face.

    "No!" I screamed, wishing my legs to move faster. "Put her down!"

    Buddy reached them first, barking and growling, hackles raised, teeth bared, ears flattened. There was no doubt he meant business.

    "You will keep your dog away from me if you know what's good for the girl," Marlon snarled, taking a few steps back.

    I stopped a few feet in front of him and raised my hands in surrender. "Put her down, Marlon. Please, please, don't hurt her."

    Kate cried softly, her eyes frantic as she tried not to move.

    I made the hand signal for Buddy to stop barking. The dog quieted but remained on high alert, his lips vibrating with the low growl coming from deep within.

    I inhaled sharply, fighting for control. "Don't do anything crazy now," I said in a surprisingly calm voice. "Just put my sister down, and let's talk about whatever the problem is."

"Whatever the problem is? Whatever the problem is?" He laughed. It was the sound of a crazy man. "The problem is your dragon, you witless boy! I know you have a dragon hidden in these woods. They only cause destruction and death, and they've ruined my life."

Kate kept her eyes locked on mine, her chin trembling with the pressure of unleashed emotions. I tried to give her a reassuring look, even though my insides churned with fear. She jerked her body, trying to free herself, but Marlon just tightened his grip.

Marlon continued, spitting as he spoke. "But you...you dare keep a dragon as a *pet!*" A vein bulged in his neck. "Dragons have taken everything from me. Everything! And I won't let that happen again—not to me or to anyone else! You call your dragon out here right now. Call it out, and I'll let the girl go."

Tears ran down Kate's face. We locked eyes, and she lightly shook her head. There was so much bravery in that little body.

When I realized there was no way out of this, it hit me like a punch to the stomach. I couldn't see an outcome that didn't involve someone getting hurt. Marlon had the power to end us, and no one would even know we were out there.

I dropped my hands in defeat and turned toward Drake's hiding place. "Drake!" I called, trying to keep my voice calm. "Drake, come!"

"No, Zander, no! Don't do it!" cried Kate, her body writhing again as she tried to break free of her captor's grip.

The trees rustled across the clearing, and Drake's green and white body appeared. He came directly toward me, just as he'd been trained to do. His uncertain gaze shifted between Marlon and me.

When he saw the dragon, Marlon's eyes grew wide. "You!" he

yelled. "You were at that barn! You killed Sam! You're supposed to be dead!" In a rage, he threw Kate to the ground and ran toward Drake, holding a knife up over his head as he let loose a guttural roar.

That's when Buddy lost it. No longer willing to stand by while his family was threatened, he chased Marlon and lunged for his leg, sinking his teeth deep into the man's flesh. Marlon screamed. His knees buckled and he fell on top of Buddy, who yelped in pain. The man growled like a wild animal as he stabbed the knife into Buddy's white fur. Screams erupted from Kate and me as we ran toward them. Drake moaned, unsure of what to do. Buddy yowled and yelped, unable to get away.

I shoved Marlon with all the fury I felt inside, knocking him off Buddy, who now lay still. Marlon jumped up, and I slammed my body into him. He tripped over a rock, and we both fell to the ground, his bloody knife falling just out of our reach.

Before I could make another move, Drake appeared. He let out a roar so loud and deep that it rattled my chest. I jumped to my feet and grabbed Kate, pulling her away from danger. Marlon scrambled back from the snarling dragon stomping ever closer to him. I had never seen such a look of terror on anyone before.

Buddy whined, catching Drake's attention. Taking advantage of the distraction, Marlon jumped up and plunged his knife into the dragon's soft white belly.

"This is for all the people you've killed!" he screamed.

Drake let out a painful wail. For a split-second, he looked down at the knife sticking out of his stomach, looked at Buddy again, and then looked at Kate and me. Then he turned toward his attacker and breathed a stream of fire.

Marlon moved just in time, so most of the fire hit the dried grass, which immediately went up in flames. The sleeve of his long coat caught fire, though, and he jumped around as he slapped at the flames. When his feet tangled, he fell and hit his head on the same rock he'd tripped over before. Marlon didn't move.

I ran to him, took my coat off, and put it over him, patting it to get the flames out. He moaned and then went silent. The dead grass around us crackled as it caught fire. Despite how much I despised this man, I wouldn't leave Marlon there to die. I grabbed his legs and dragged his limp body safely from the flames. I grabbed my coat and put it on, ignoring the smell of soot.

Kate screamed as Drake fell to the ground. I went to the dragon, and Kate crawled to Buddy.

Blood oozed from Drake's wound. I carefully pulled the knife from his belly and threw it into the burning grass. Putting my hand on his bloody injury, I shook my head as I struggled to speak. "Drake," I whispered. "Oh, Drake." There were no words to express what I felt. Tears flowed down my cheeks. He looked at me with a gentleness that relayed everything we two had ever felt about each other.

Buddy let out a slow, breathy whine. Despite Drake's injury, the dragon pulled away from me and slowly crawled over to his best friend. The dog lay on his side, dark red spreading over his thick white fur. His belly slowly rose and fell.

Kate knelt next to the dog. "Please be okay. Please be okay," she cried. She pressed her hands on his wounds to stop the bleeding, but there were too many. Her tears mixed with the dog's blood. "Don't leave us, Buddy. We need you here." She sobbed openly. Her pain couldn't be held back.

I knelt beside my dog, softly stroking his head the way he always liked. Seeing how badly he was injured, I knew he wouldn't survive. I looked up at Kate, tears still running down my face. "He's hurt real bad, Kate."

"No, don't say it!" she wailed.

"He's…he's not going to make it," I said softly, struggling to get the words out.

I couldn't believe this was happening. He was more than just a dog; he was my best friend, my secret keeper, my buddy. The thought of a world without him in my life was too big, too empty.

I gently stroked his fur, trying to offer him some comfort—to be there with him, like he had always been there for me.

He released a soft whine as he intently looked into my eyes. His breaths grew more shallow, each one taking more effort than the last.

As my heart broke, I whispered, "It's okay, Buddy. I know you need to go. You've earned your rest. Thank you for being such a brave dog. So very brave. I love you." A gasping sob pushed out of my throat as I kissed my best friend goodbye.

Drake moaned and gently nuzzled the dog with his snout. Buddy lifted his head just enough to take one more look at his family. Then he laid his head on the ground, closed his eyes, and let out his final breath.

"No, Buddy! Please, no!" Kate cried, throwing her body over him.

Drake let out a long pain-filled wail and collapsed onto his side. Crouching next to the dragon, I put my hand on the wound again to try to stop the blood flow, but there was too much. It quickly seeped through my fingers. Drake closed his eyes and moaned softly, laying his head on the ground close to Buddy's.

"Kate!" I called out, needing to be heard over her sobs. "Give me something to stop the bleeding. Help me!" It was enough to bring her out of her hysteria.

She knelt beside me and wiped her face, which left her cheeks streaked with blood. She took off her heavy coat and the sweater she'd worn over her shirt, handing the sweater to me. "Use this. Press it hard against the hole." She put her coat back on and watched as I did what she said. Drake moaned again.

"I'm sorry, Drake," I whispered. "I know it hurts. Just hang in there. Please!"

Kate drew in a sharp breath. She shook my shoulder and pointed to the fire. The flames had been hungrily consuming the dead grass in the clearing and now filled the air with the bitter stench of smoke. The wind blew sparks across the field, away from us.

"We should be safe from the fire for now. The wind's blowing it the other way," I told her. "We need something big enough to wrap around him to hold your sweater in place."

She looked around us. "We don't have anything." Her voice held a trace of panic. "I don't know what to do!"

Just then, I heard the beat of horses' hooves. My breath caught as Antony rode into the meadow with two knights right behind him.

Chapter 26

A ntony called out, "What's going on here? We saw the smoke from inside the city walls." When he saw Drake lying near us, he yelled, "Get back, you two!" He leaped off his horse and instantly unsheathed his sword, taking long steps toward us with his weapon pointed at the dragon.

I stepped in his path, carefully avoiding the tip of the sword. "No, Antony, it's all right. He's ours."

He blinked rapidly. "What do you mean, he's yours? That's a dragon!"

The two knights behind Antony exchanged wary looks. I called out to them. "I need you two to find Red and Luca, the boys who work in the stables with me. Bring them here. And tell them to find Nyla. She needs to bring all her medical supplies, especially wraps. We need everything she has." The men didn't move. "Well, don't just stand there." I pointed in the direction of the city. "Go!"

Antony nodded his approval to the knights and added, "And bring some other men with you. We must put out this fire."

They turned their horses and galloped across the clearing, disappearing into the trees.

"I think he's going to be all right," Kate said to me, her hands still pressed on Drake's wound. "See? His eyes look better already."

I hurried to Drake's side, relieved to see his eyes open and alert. "Drake, old friend. Stay with us. We need you." I knew Drake wouldn't understand me but hoped my tone would be enough to keep him calm.

Antony stood unmoving, sword still drawn. "A dragon? I don't understand. You've been—what—*friends* with a dragon all this time and never told us?" His voice grew louder as he spoke. "Do you realize that this dragon is an enemy of Trulith?"

He stepped closer to me. Reaching my arm out to stop Antony, I kept my eyes on Drake as I spoke, hoping it would help my voice remain calm. "Antony, this is Drake. Decades ago, he was injured while protecting my great-great-grandfather from a bear attack. So, my family took him in, healed him, trained him, and welcomed him as part of our family. Drake is an amazing creature who can do incredible things." I stroked the dragon's neck.

Hearing his name, Drake turned toward me and blinked his eyes slowly. Kate continued applying pressure to his wound.

"But...but it's a dragon!" Antony shook his sword for emphasis.

I turned to him. "Please, put away your sword and come closer. He's not like other dragons. You'll see that Drake has no desire to harm you."

Antony came a little closer but continued to hold his sword. Drake trained his eyes on the knight, and I hoped the dragon stayed calm despite Antony's aggressive behavior.

"But what he did to our city..."

"No, Antony. I promise Drake had nothing to do with any of the attacks. In fact, during that last attack, Kate and I were here in the forest with him. He saved the whole kingdom by calling out to the dragons during the last attack."

"That sound—that was him?"

I nodded. "I don't know what he said to them, but they left immediately. Drake is Trulith's defender, not its attacker. He is no enemy to the kingdom."

Antony tilted his head and stood quietly for a moment. Sighing, he finally put his sword in its sheath. "What happened over there?" he asked, pointing to the fire. "Are you going to tell me the fire started on its own? Wait, what is that off to the side? Is that—is that a body?"

"That's Marlon," I said. "I pulled him out of the path of the fire."

"Is he okay? Is he alive?" Antony asked over his shoulder as he hurried to the unmoving body.

I followed him. "He's alive. He conked his head pretty hard on a rock when he fell, though, and he hasn't woken up."

Antony knelt down, checking Marlon's neck for a pulse. Satisfied, he gently lifted Marlon's arm to check his burns. "That will need medical aid," Antony said. He stood and put his hands on his hips as he looked over the clearing. "We must get that fire contained," he said. "Your dragon is to blame for it, I assume."

"Um, yes, sir, but it was in defense against Marlon." I told him what happened, ending with, "and I believe Marlon was responsible for the death of our father several months ago. He and another man attacked him when they tried to get to Drake."

Antony locked eyes with me for a moment, as if deciding if he should believe me. He said nothing but walked across the scorched remnants of grass. Using a handkerchief, he picked up Marlon's knife, now black and smoking from the fire.

"That's Marlon's," Kate said, the anger in her voice unmistakable. "He used it to kill our dog and stab our dragon." Her breath hitched.

Antony tucked the knife into his belt. "I'll keep this, then." I took a breath, ready to defend my dragon from any further accusations, but Antony stopped me with a wave of his hand. "You don't need to say any more. I'd heard stories of Marlon's mind not being right, and what you've told me supports those stories. That man was obsessed with hunting dragons. I'm very sorry his actions had such terrible consequences for your family." He glanced at Drake and then at Buddy. "I truly am sorry."

"Drake and Buddy were best friends, if you can imagine that," I told Antony. "They were part of our family and loved playing together." Tears fell down my cheeks once again. It seemed I had a never-ending supply of tears.

The sound of horse hooves announced the arrival of a group of knights. Antony went to speak with them. One dismounted while another rode to Marlon's unmoving body. Antony and the other knight lifted Marlon onto the saddle in front of the rider, and the horse hurried off toward Trulith. The other knights dismounted and secured their horses safely away from the fire. Antony joined them and, together, they shoveled dirt onto the flames.

I watched the smoke swirl upward, blending with the sky, and in my heart, I pictured Buddy's spirit ascending, now free to jump and run with endless joy.

Chapter 27

Our friends soon arrived on horseback and quickly dismounted. Nyla helped Dora get down from the horse they shared. They all stopped short when they saw the scene before them. Dora yelped and hid behind Nyla.

Red was the first to speak, pointing at Drake. "Zander, that's a…that's a…"

"Dragon," I finished for him as I approached my friends. "Yes, it is. His name is Drake, and he's been a part of my family for generations." I wasn't surprised by the fearful looks on their faces but kept my voice calm. "He came to Trulith with us and has been living hidden in this forest ever since."

"So, when you and Kate would disappear…," Luca started.

I nodded. "That's when we visited Drake. We didn't tell anyone about him because we thought it would be safer for everyone if we kept him a secret."

Luca scowled. "People died because of the dragon attacks. My friend *died*!" He pointed at Drake. "And you've been keeping him here?"

I gently squeezed Luca's shoulder and tried to reassure him. "I promise, Drake was not involved in the attacks. He actually ended the last one when he called out to the dragons and made them leave."

"But…," Luca started.

Kate spoke up. "There are good dragons and there are bad dragons. Drake's a good dragon, and he's my friend."

Luca pressed his lips together, falling silent as his gaze shifted between the dragon and us. After a moment, he offered a subtle nod.

Nyla saw Kate holding the bloody sweater against Drake's belly. "Oh, he's injured," Nyla said, kneeling on the other side, seemingly unconcerned that she was so close to a dragon. She opened her satchel of medical supplies. "I've only worked on humans before. Oh, listen to me," she chuckled nervously. "I've never even seen a dragon up close." She let out a breath but saw Kate's concerned face and gave her a smile of encouragement. "But don't worry, Kate. We'll figure this out together." She pulled out several large rolls of bandages as Dora bravely stood next to Nyla to watch.

With Drake being taken care of and the fire almost extinguished, I knelt next to my dog's lifeless body. I gently stroked a section of soft white fur that was unstained by blood. I didn't care that I was crying in front of the others. I let the tears flow as I mourned the loss of this brave, smart, caring dog I'd known for most of my life.

Red and Luca knelt beside me. I felt an arm wrap around my shoulders in support. I hiccupped as I talked through my tears. "He died saving Drake's life."

Luca sniffed and wiped his cheek with the back of his hand. "Buddy was a great dog, Zander. One of a kind." He sniffed again, stood, and took a few steps back as he rubbed his eyes.

"I'm so sorry," Red said quietly. He patted my back before

walking to the knights who had extinguished the fire. He came back a moment later, shovel in hand. "Let's bury him, so he can rest in peace."

I nodded and wiped my face with my sleeves. "Over there," I pointed. "Bury him there. That's where we entered the meadow, where Buddy always yipped with excitement when he'd see Drake." I smiled shakily.

Red dug the hole. When he returned, he said softly, "I can carry him over there if you want me to."

"No, I'll do it," I whispered, my throat tight with emotion. Kate had been listening, her face showing her immense grief. I cleared my throat. "Kate, it's time to say goodbye."

Her chin quivered as she knelt beside me, her eyes pooling with tears. She buried her face in the dog's neck and wept openly. After a moment, she grew quieter. "You saved our lives. You're the bravest dog in the whole world, and I'll never, ever forget you," she whispered. She kissed his head and sat up, wiping her face. "'Bye, Buddy."

I took a deep breath as I tried to gather what remained of my withering emotional strength. Lifting Buddy's lifeless body from the ground, I held him close to my chest. "You were the best, Buddy, the absolute best," I whispered.

I carried him to Drake, who sat up slightly as I approached. He lifted his front foot and rubbed it repeatedly along the dog's side, petting Buddy just like a human would do. I brought him closer, and Drake nuzzled his snout against his best friend for the last time. A low, sorrowful moan escaped the dragon, and his eyes filled with tears before his injured body collapsed to the ground in exhaustion and pain.

Nyla and Dora wept openly as I carried Buddy to the newly dug grave. With great care, I lowered Buddy into the ground and let my fingers sink into his soft fur in a final caress. Kate and I stood beside the hole as Red gently covered the hero's body with dirt.

"I'm gonna miss him so much," Kate whispered as she held my hand.

"Me, too, sweet girl. Me, too."

After a quiet moment, we wiped our tears and joined the others who were gathered near our injured dragon.

I cleared my throat, trying to speak through my grief. "Thank you, all of you, for your help tonight. Kate and I have experienced so much death, so much loss. In the past, we had to go through most of that alone." I paused and took a deep breath before I continued. "It helps now that we have people who care."

With a wobbly smile, Nyla said, "You're our family. We're here for you." She took a cleansing breath. "I think the dragon will be okay. He just needs time to heal. Kate and I have bandaged him tightly. His wound isn't nearly as bad as it might have been. His thick hide kept the knife from going in too far. If he leaves it alone, his injury should be healed in a week or so, if he gets the rest he needs." Nyla looked around the group. "Now the question is: where will he stay while he recuperates?"

Kate knelt beside Drake who reached out and touched her for a long moment. She spoke softly. "He wants to stay here. This is his home—the forest and the meadow. That way, he can be near Buddy, too," she whispered, almost to herself. She looked for my approval, which I gave with a nod.

"I can come out and check on him at times, if you think, uh, Drake would be okay with that," Red offered. He looked a little nervous about his suggestion, but I was pleased with his willingness to help.

"I'll come out each day to check his bandage," Nyla offered, "and, Kate, maybe you would like to come with me. I could use the help."

Kate nodded.

"Me, too," said Dora quietly.

Nyla put an arm around Dora's shoulder. "Yes, and you, too."

Luca also offered his assistance, which I knew was a big gesture of friendship, considering his hatred of dragons.

Antony approached us, and I hesitantly looked up at him, afraid of what he would say. He could demand we turn over Drake to them. But I wouldn't give him up without a fight. If it came to that, I was ready to defend my friend—my family.

Antony bit his lower lip as he looked at our group. "You say the dragon isn't a threat to Trulith's citizens." He looked directly at me. "I will hold you to that. If this dragon causes any harm, we will have him killed. Do you understand?"

I nodded. I had expected no less.

"That being said, it sounds like he's the hero of Trulith's last attack, and I owe him and you our deepest gratitude."

"Th-thank you, Antony," I stammered. "I don't know what to say."

"Tend to your family. You all have the day off from work tomorrow. Use it as a day to grieve, to rest, and to make a future plan."

"A future plan, sir?" I asked.

He squeezed my shoulder. "Your dragon can't stay hidden in this forest forever, Zander. If someone came across him out here, there would be a massive uproar. We'll give him time to recover from his wound, but then you'll need to come up with a plan for where he'll live. Might I suggest the Dragon Sanctuary?"

"The Dragon Sanctuary? What's that?" I asked, hopeful for a good solution to our problem.

"Our new gardener, Binobrik, mentioned it to me. He said it's a place where dragons are kept safe, and where injured dragons can heal."

Kate squealed. "Drake could go there!"

"Kate, honey, he won't be able to fly until his wound is better," Nyla said.

Antony continued, "We've also heard talk of the Dragon Army being assembled in the far east of Illusia. Some of its dragons are chosen from the Sanctuary. If Drake is chosen, it would be an amazing honor."

I asked, "How do we find out more about this Dragon Sanctuary?"

"I'll ask Binobrik for more information, and I'll get back to you. I assure you that my knights and I will keep your dragon's existence quiet for now. Just keep him out of sight." With that, Antony and his knights mounted their horses and returned to the city.

After bedding down Drake in a secure spot, we all returned home, two on each horse. Even though my heart was filled with grief and worries, I was grateful that we had friends to help us through this.

Chapter 28

Drake's healing progressed just as Nyla had hoped. Everyone helped like they said they would, and the dragon was checked on at least twice a day. Kate and I also visited every day to remind him of our love for him.

"He's getting better, but he looks sad," Kate said. She held my hand as we walked home after a visit.

"Yes, he does. I think he misses Buddy."

"I miss him, too." Her last word became a wail as her grief broke free from her little body.

I stopped, bent down, and pulled her into a hug, which she returned fiercely.

Once her shoulders stopped shaking from her sobbing, I took her hands in mine, rubbing her knuckles with my calloused thumbs. "Buddy loved you very much," I whispered, swallowing the lump in my throat. "He knew you loved him, too. He was a brave dog who gave his life to keep his family safe. So, it's okay to feel sad or mad or whatever you feel." I tucked a loose strand of hair behind her ear, and she wiped her nose with her sleeve.

"Kate, you have a heart of gold, just like Ma did. You make people feel good about themselves. You've always done that for me, and now other people need that from you, too. Drake needs your pretty smile to help him feel better. Nyla needs your help to heal the sick. Dora needs you to be her friend. I need you, and I always will, because you are my true family. We have great memories with Buddy, and it's okay to be sad that he's gone, but we also need to be happy that we had him in our lives. I think we should do what Ma said and choose joy."

She wore a trembling smile as she nodded. "Choose joy."

After Drake had fully healed from his knife wound, we tried to get him to play, but he refused. It hurt my heart that he didn't seem to care if we came to visit him, but I understood. A big part of his life was missing now. The thing that brought him the most joy was gone. His physical injury had healed, but his heart hadn't.

"Maybe it's because we always brought Buddy with us, and now we can't," Kate suggested.

She was right. When Drake saw us coming, he always expected Buddy to come yipping across the meadow. Kate and I had become a constant reminder of the loss of his best friend.

So, it wasn't surprising when Drake took a particular interest in the next dragon attack. Kate and I happened to be visiting him when the Trulith warning horn sounded, alerting its citizens of the dragons' presence once again. We ran to the edge of the woods, with Drake close behind.

"They're back," Kate whispered fearfully. All of the dragons were here this time: the dark red dragon, the big green one, two brown ones, and the two smaller ones. "That's a lot of dragons."

We watched from the forest as the big dragons caused mayhem. Some landed on the shiny roofs briefly before becoming airborne again while others flew through the city, flames and smoke billowing in their wake.

Drake moaned and shuffled back and forth, looking more miserable than I had ever seen him. He kept his eyes on the attacking dragons.

Kate looked up at me with tears in her eyes. "I think he wants to go with them. To *be* with them." Her voice quivered. "We need to tell him it's okay to go."

I gently squeezed her shoulder. "Are you sure? We might not ever see him again."

"But he'd be with his own kind. He'd be happy. Drake needs his own family, like we've found our own. That's more important than keeping him here with us. And maybe he can stop them from ever attacking people again."

She was right. And now that Marlon and the others knew about him, this place wasn't safe for Drake anymore.

"Binobrik told me where he believes the Dragon Sanctuary is. Do you think I can touch Drake and he'll understand my thoughts, like he can do to us?"

Kate's face lit up. "It can't hurt to try. If he can get to that Sanctuary place, he would be safe. Please try."

Kate and I stepped in Drake's path. He stopped pacing and got down on all fours, looking at us with tender eyes.

I touched Drake's head and filled my mind with thoughts about the Dragon Sanctuary. Drake jerked his head away from my hand, surprise showing in his eyes.

"It's okay," I said softly as I nodded. He allowed me to put my hand back on his head, and I continued sending my thoughts to him. I tried to relay to him how to get there and that it was a place where he would be safe. I ran through everything three times, hoping it was enough to make him understand. I stepped back, and Drake gave me a look of understanding.

"I think it worked," I said to Kate. A moment passed between us, filled only with the sound of our breathing. Finally, I said, "I guess it's time to say goodbye."

Kate let out a sob as we both hugged our big friend. When we stepped back, he tilted his head to the side, questioning us.

I took a deep breath, pointed to the sky, and said, "Drake, go." The dragon narrowed his eyes as he looked at me and then at the direction I was pointing. Tears slid down my cheeks, but I continued pointing. I nodded repeatedly and again said, "Drake, go."

Kate took a wavering breath. "It's okay," she said to him, trying to smile encouragingly despite her quivering lips. "Go. Be with the other dragons. Take them to the Dragon Sanctuary. They'll be your family now."

Drake looked above the city, watching the other dragons, then looked back at us—his friends, his family. He closed his eyes for a moment and lowered his head. He stepped toward us and, with the gentlest of motions, he rubbed the side of his snout against Kate's arm. She wrapped her arms around his neck, hugging him fiercely as she wept. The air filled with the sound of a little girl whose heart was breaking...again. After a moment, she gasped and pulled away. She nodded at Drake.

Then he turned to me and leaned his forehead against mine, just as he had done so many times before. With his touch, my mind saw Drake's happy memories with our family, some I didn't even know about. And then he showed me his plan: he would guide the dragons to the Sanctuary, and if they wouldn't go with him, he would go alone.

"Yes," I whispered as I reached my arms around his neck. I felt his powerful body lean on me, like a returned hug. I had never imagined there would be a time when Drake wouldn't be a part of my life, a part of my family.

My chest ached. Once again, I had to say goodbye to someone I loved.

So many goodbyes.

But this one was different. This one was by choice, and I knew deep down that it was the right thing to do.

"I love you, boy." I stepped back, pointed to the sky again, and nodded. "Drake, go."

Our dragon took one last meaningful look at both of us, gave a short whisper of a whine, and flapped his wings. As he became airborne, he called out to the dragons with a sound like the one he had used to end the previous attack. The dragons immediately rose higher in the sky and turned in his direction. The giant red one returned his call. Drake flew toward them, and I had to fight every desire inside me that wanted to call him back.

Kate buried her face in my shirt, holding on with a strong grip as she cried. Drake circled back to us, floating low in the air. He hovered in front of us and, with a low moan, said his final goodbye. I raised a hand in farewell, and Kate pulled her face from my shirt for one last look.

"Be good, Drake. We love you," she called, blowing him a kiss.

Drake closed his eyes and lowered his head for a moment, wings pumping gently. Then he turned toward the city. He let out another sound, and the dragons flew away, Drake staying lower to the ground while the others soared high.

"Goodbye, old friend," I whispered. I never knew it was possible to feel pain and joy at the same time.

After a moment, Kate said softly, "Now Drake has a whole world to explore. He chose joy."

My heart felt heavy as my mind flickered through the difficulties of the past year—Pa's death, losing our home, Kate being struck by lightning, Buddy's death, and now Drake leaving us. But as I watched my friend's form become smaller and smaller in the distance, I realized that, despite all the bad things we'd endured, each one had led to good things, too. We had a new family, I had a job so I could take care of Kate, and I had a heart full of happy memories I could revisit whenever I wanted.

I took a deep breath and smiled through my tears.

I chose joy.

Hey there, adventurous reader!

Thanks for reading! Want some **free digital art**? Go to dianemartinbooks.com/drake and follow the instructions to receive an original full-color digital file of Drake with the butterfly on his nose. It's only available to my newsletter subscribers, which is also how you can be the first to know about my upcoming books.

If you enjoyed THE DRAGON KEEPER, **please leave a review** on Amazon and other online stores, tell your friends, and ask your school and city libraries to carry it. Those are the best ways to help me as an author. Spread the word!

Have you read the book that came before this—THE GEM KEEPER? Binobrik, the quirky gardening gnome, plays a big role in that story. I'm sure you'll love it!

The next book in this series is THE DRAGON SANCTUARY, which, as you know, is where Drake is headed. He appears in future books of THE ILLUSIA CHRONICLES, but you'll have to keep reading the series to find out more!

Scan the QR code below to be taken directly to my website (dianemartinbooks.com), where you can learn all about my middle-grade fantasy adventure novels.

Acknowledgments

I want to extend special thanks to my early readers and critique partners: Dan Buckhout, Caroline Yu, Laura Stegman, Toni Short, Lori Owen, Tonda Lee, and Amanda Helm. Thanks also to Dr. Joe Norton for editing an early version of The Dragon Keeper; all errors are mine.

I have massive appreciation for Josh Martin who once drew a comical picture of a butterfly on a dragon's snout, which jump-started my imagination for the butterfly scenes and, eventually, for this entire novel. He also created this beautiful cover and the amazing illustrations. (Just wait until you see what's coming in the remaining books of this series!)

Some may think this is silly, but I want to give a shout out to Cher, our white Husky-mix rescue dog, who was the inspiration for Buddy. I cried as I wrote Buddy's death scene because our Cher is old, and her remaining time with us is limited. She has been a joy to have in our family. Thank you, Cher Bear, for being you.

About Us

Diane Martin is a writer of middle-grade fantasy adventures. She has been married forever and left the corporate accounting life to raise her four kids—three knights and one princess; they're all grown now and having their own adventures. Diane loves stories with fantasy, superheroes, or a post-apocalyptic setting. She lives in Texas with her husband and two "old lady" rescue dogs.

Josh Martin, the illustrator, loves to create cool things using his imagination. He has a degree in digital art and currently uses his artistic skills in three different ways: as the artist for a video game developer, as a children's book illustrator, and as a middle-school art teacher. Josh lives in Texas with his wife and daughter.

Made in the USA
Coppell, TX
05 October 2024